IN HIS GOOD HANDS

THE BRIDES OF PURPLE HEART RANCH BOOK 9

SHANAE JOHNSON

THOSE JOHNSON GIRLS

Copyright © 2019, Ines Johnson. All rights reserved.
This novel is a work of fiction. All characters, places, and incidents described in this publication are used fictitiously, or are entirely fictional. No part of this publication may be reproduced or transmitted, in any form or by any means, except by an authorized retailer, or with written permission of the author.

Edited by Alyssa Breck

Manufactured in the United States of America
First Edition October 2019

CHAPTER ONE

"My grandfather was in the military."

"Mine, too." Corporal Colin Chase grinned down at the freckle-faced young man standing at his table. Good, thought Chase. This was an excellent start. Historically, kids with military members in their families were more likely to enlist.

"But not my dad," said the kid. He made a fan of the glossy pamphlets on the exhibit table and then shoved them all back into a single queue. "He thought military service was a waste of time and too dangerous. He decided to start a business instead."

Chase didn't repeat the *mine too* this time, even though this kid was narrating his life.

"But the business failed a couple of years ago," the kid continued, "and we had to move back in with my grandparents."

Chase winced. Not at the thought of living with

his grandfather. Moving in with his grandfather would've been a delight for him as a kid. His grandfather had been his idol even after his death a few years ago. What was cringe-worthy was the idea of moving back in with his parents. It was absolutely unthinkable for Chase.

Luckily, Chase's grandfather had made sure he would never have to do that. General Charles Chase had left his grandson a healthy trust, which Chase had never needed to touch. What Chase had reached for instead was following in his grandfather's footsteps of serving his country in the Armed Forces.

"I've always thought about serving," the kid was saying. "But my mom wants me to go to college."

"No reason you can't do both," said Chase. "The Army offers excellent education benefits and job training."

"Yeah?" The young man's voice raised an octave as he scratched at the tiny hairs on his chin.

Chase couldn't hide his smile. He just knew the Army could make a man out of this boy. He was a perfect candidate. He hadn't made a single comparison to the military and video games, meaning he had some level of maturity. He hadn't asked Chase how many people he'd killed, meaning he wasn't a psychopath. And he'd wandered over to the table without being corralled.

Yes, here was an excellent prospect. Chase just

needed to close the deal. He had never thought he'd be a salesman. That was his father's realm. But in this, recruiting for the service, Chase was selling something he believed in.

Even before his years in the Army, Chase could've sat on his rump and lived off his family's money. Instead, he'd wanted to do something important with his life. His years in the service had accomplished that.

Unfortunately, Chase was no longer able to go into combat with his injuries. But he didn't want to leave the service. This new job of recruiting young men and women into the service was the perfect new career for him. However, there were drawbacks.

"Timothy." An older woman yanked at the elbow of Chase's young prospect. "The recruiter from the university wants to talk to you."

"I'll be over in a minute, Mom," said Timothy.

Timothy's mother pinched her mouth in that universal language of mothers that said *do what I say before you get a spanking.* "He doesn't have much time. He'll be leaving soon. You should go now."

Timothy clearly read mom-speak. He huffed, but he obeyed his mom. "All right. I'm going."

Chase offered the young man his hand before he could step away. "Think about what I said, Timothy, and take my card."

His mother's hand snatched the card before

Timothy's fingers could reach it. "Oh, I'll take that, honey. You go on now, the recruiter's waiting."

Timothy gave Chase a nod. The kid turned on his heel and headed over to the other side of the room, where the state college booths were set up.

Chase braced himself on the table. His palms touched down on the recruitment pamphlets, spreading them out into a fan, like a front line defense. He steeled himself for the attack to come.

Timothy's mother turned to him with a smile. It was genuine. They always were.

"Thank you for your service," said the woman. "But I'll thank you to keep your hands off my son."

With a glare that rivaled his own mother's, the woman turned and walked to her son, who was shaking the hand of the college recruiter.

A pulsing knot began at the base of Chase's skull. The headache was dull, but he got the feeling it would persist for the rest of the day.

Chase collected the pamphlets into a single queue. Not a single one of the glossy brochures had left the table today. He could understand parents being protective of their children. But, on the whole, the military wasn't any more dangerous than a college campus. In fact, he was sure there was more danger at a frat house or a college tailgate than at a base.

"Another one bites the dust?"

Chase turned to his partner in crime.

Mark Ortega's dimpled grin was grim as he eyed their empty table. His gaze lifted to the kids and parents meandering around the many college and trade school booths. "Looks like the college got him instead."

"I was so close to closing that kid," said Chase. "He's exactly what the service needs."

The kid leaned into the college recruiter. His mother patted him on the back encouragingly. The card Chase had given her slipped from her fingers as her kid shook the recruiter's hand.

Chase didn't begrudge the kid for getting an education. But couldn't his mother see that in the military he could do both and come out ahead? As a vet, Timothy would've come into the workforce with proven skills and leadership experience. And no debt.

"How many does that make for us today?" asked Ortega.

"A big fat goose egg," moaned Chase.

"And for the week?"

"Two."

The corners of Ortega's mouth lowered into a grimace. "Well, those stats at least put us on par with the national average."

Chase blew out a harsh breath. The national average for recruitment was down by the thousands. Chase was used to succeeding. He did not like to be anywhere but at the front of the pack, and now he was lagging behind.

"If we could just get into the schools again, we could get our numbers up." Chase dumped the pamphlets into a carrying container.

"Fat chance," said Ortega as he folded the table. "I can't get any guidance counselors to return my calls. And the one time we did go this year, students met with an anti-war protest."

Even now, they had been relegated to the back corner of the post-secondary fair. The only reason people had come to visit their table was for the raffle of a new pair of wireless earbuds. No one had actually stayed up to chat. They all thanked him for his service.

"Let's get out of here."

Chase was ready to go, but he wasn't giving up. The two men had spent half the day at this college and career fair sponsored by the city. They could head back to the recruitment center and make those phone calls. At some point, someone had to pick up.

In fact, Ortega was doing just that. The moment they stepped out of the doors, a blonde woman threw herself at Ortega. Mark dropped the table and scooped up his wife.

"Hey, Honey. What are you doing here?"

Honey Ortega's bright eyes lit as she gazed down at her husband. Chase would've sworn he saw red hearts coming out of her eyelids.

"I told you," said Honey, "my sister's speaking. Hey, Colin."

Chase forgot his manners. His ears perked at the mention of Honey's sister. Prickled was more like it. The last thing he wanted to do was to run into her. Ginger Dumasse was one of the reasons he was having trouble recruiting.

"Education, tech jobs, higher minimum wages, these are the wave of the future for our city."

Too late.

Her authoritative voice carried over the speakers set up in the courtyard. The woman didn't need the amplifier. Her very presence made everyone stand up and take notice.

Strawberry-blonde hair. A defiant chin. Square shoulders. Chase couldn't help but stare. How could someone so breathtakingly beautiful be so rigid?

Her gaze caught his. Did he imagine it, or did her breath catch in a gasp? Did he fantasize it, or did her nostrils flare? In the next blink of his eyes, wide blue eyes narrowed, and perfect lips pinched in distaste.

Ginger Dumasse leaned into the microphone and proclaimed, "College should be the first push for all youth."

Yup, it had been a figment of Chase's imagination. Ginger Dumasse clearly stood on the opposite side of the way from Chase on the issue of higher education versus military experience. Among other things.

Around him, parents nodded their heads in agreement with her.

"That's why I intend to invest in your children's future if elected. I'm a warrior for this state. I'll do it with nothing but my wits. I'm a sharpshooter, be it with a firearm or a pen."

The audience whooped and applauded at those choice words.

"My aim is perfect. And what I'm fighting for is to become your next state senator."

Applause boomed. He didn't agree with her, but her speech was rousing enough that his hands itched to add to the applause. Too bad his hands were full of his own interests. Chase hefted the container of pamphlets and turned to his car.

CHAPTER TWO

Ginger lived for this. She lived for the podium, for the talking points, for the questions, even for the defiance.

"What are you going to do about the C&C Factory moving jobs out of state?"

She had notes in front of her, but she didn't need them. Ginger spoke from her heart because that's where her ideas came from, that's where her platform had been built.

"That is a shell company from out of state. I know many in the community are employed there, but I'm a firm believer in investing in our community with neighbors who own businesses here. We can't expect others to do it. We must become self-reliant. That's why I have a plan to give tax incentives to local businesses and startups."

She watched as the man took a deep breath. His

head tilted back, and his gaze squinted. She didn't have him yet. She knew why.

People didn't want talking points, they didn't want politics. They just wanted someone with a solid plan that reflected their needs. She had loads of those.

It wasn't an immediate solution. It would take time for her plan to work. But people needed relief now.

Ginger opened her mouth to win the voter over, but her heart skipped. She didn't shake. She never choked. But she did take a moment to swallow the excess saliva in her throat.

He was staring at her. Not the voter. Well, the voter was staring because he was waiting for her to continue on her stump. But behind him was a tall, thick-limbed, oak tree of a man.

Sergeant Colin Chase glared at her.

Did she imagine it, or was there a softness to his stern features? Did she fantasize it, or did his lips part? Dark brown eyes narrowed, and his kissable lips pinched in disapproval.

Yup, it had been a figment of her imagination.

Chase had thrown her off her game. And he saw that he had. He might have big muscles, chiseled cheekbones, and a gaze that pierced right through her. But she had the megaphone.

"What you all really want to know is why you should vote for me over an incumbent of twenty-five years. It's not because I'm younger with fresh ideas, although that's true. It's not because I'm a woman, and you want to show progress, although that's not a faulty idea since women are rising business owners and gaining more wealth."

For his part, Chase raised a brow and turned to leave. Her heart thudded again. This time it left behind an empty, hollow feeling. She didn't want him to leave. She wanted him to stay and fight, to argue with her. She ached to prove him wrong. But she couldn't do that if he was walking away from her.

Someone cleared their throat. Ginger turned to look at her campaign manager, Carla, who was also her best friend. Carla raised a perfectly trimmed brow with meaning.

Ginger turned back to the sea of faces waiting for her next bit of speech. She pulled on a smile. What was she supposed to say? It was all Chase's fault. He'd distracted her.

She pulled the cards from her pocket. She looked down at her notes. The documents were all out of order. No matter. She knew what was in her heart.

"You should vote for me because, at my core, I believe we should all live in a world that is fair and just. It should be that way in our families, in our work environment, and in our government. It doesn't matter what interest groups or red tape come at me.

That's who I am at my core. If that's you, then I'm the candidate for you."

There was a moment of uncertainty. Then the crowd broke off in applause and whoops and cheers for *Dumasse.*

She'd done it. She'd won them over. Just a few more thousands to go.

"That wasn't in your speech," said Carla as Ginger came down off the podium.

"It was in my heart," insisted Ginger.

"Cute. Let's put that in your stump. It's playing well with the suburbanites and industry workers."

Ginger loved her bestie. Carla had majored in political science, where Ginger had majored in graphic design. A fat lot of good it did her.

A year out of college, Carla had talked Ginger into doing pro bono work for her first campaign. The client, a local mayoral candidate, had a message that captured both Ginger's imagination and her interest. Ginger designed posters for the candidate, only to realize she wanted to say the slogans she was designing.

She ran for local office the next election cycle and won a seat on the city council. Now she was ready for the big leagues. There was so much more she could do as a state senator.

"The polls are still showing you down amongst housewives and males," Carla said as she tapped on her tablet.

Argh. Ginger hated the polls. But if she wanted to win, she had to listen to them.

"Voters don't trust your unmarried status."

"Well, I'm not getting a husband just to win an election." Ginger shuddered.

She wanted a husband. Some day. But the qualifications for her partner were high. He'd need to be man enough to contend with a woman in power. And let's face it, there weren't many of those around.

"You don't need a husband, per se," said Carla. "You could just date until after the election."

Ginger stopped walking. They'd been down this road. She had no plans to take a single step in the direction her best friend was suggesting.

Carla shrugged, still tapping away at her handheld. "There was a lot of interest when you were linked with a certain sergeant"

Two months ago, Ginger had been photographed in the arms of Sergeant Colin Chase. It had been innocent. Not like he'd kissed her or anything. Even though he might have stared at her lips. But he didn't do anything about it.

"Isn't he here today?" Carla looked up finally.

"He's gone."

Ginger bit her lip when she realized her mistake. But it was too late. Carla was grinning the smug grin she'd worn when she'd gotten the highest score in the Psychology 101 class.

"What?" shrugged Ginger. "I saw him with Honey. I was checking on my little sister."

"Hmmm." That was the sound Carla had made when she'd gotten the highest grade in their Sociology 101 class.

"It would never work between us. We're on the opposite ends of ... well, everything."

"Isn't that what your whole platform is about? Bringing two sides together."

Ginger rolled her eyes. "Don't we have real issues to talk about?"

And not the nonsense of dating a sergeant who couldn't even offer her a smile today. Or anytime they'd been breathing the same air.

It didn't matter. She didn't need his appreciation. She was a strong, confident, independent woman.

Even if when she'd been in his arms for that brief moment, her strong back had gone to goo.

CHAPTER THREE

"Ellie Wilson," said the announcer.

The young man in question winced as he climbed the stairs of the stage. The announcer had butchered Eli's name, but his parents still applauded. Their applause was amplified by the two teams of soldiers, the soldiers' wives, and the ranch children taking up an entire wing of the audience in the gymnasium.

Of course, the soldiers of the Purple Heart Ranch were all here. Once anyone set foot on the ranch, they were treated as family. And the soldiers took care of their own, including becoming a cheering section for this year's senior graduates.

Chase's time on the ranch was up. He had moved out three weeks ago. But that didn't stop the guys from coming over to his place, the wives sending him off with food, and everyone still nosing in his business. Even though he lived in town now, he was on the ranch five days a week. Sometimes every day. It was as though nothing had changed.

"Billy Trent."

The soldiers hooted and hollered louder than the kid's blood family. Billy had come to them an uncoordinated mess. Now, he marched up the stairs to the stage with his back straight and his head high.

The same happened with Ayden Benson and Jordan Scott. The cadets of the JROTC program of the Purple Heart Ranch were each walking across the stage. Every one of them was decked out with academic and service honors.

Those two had been destined for factory work. Which was admirable. Chase knew many of their family members worked in the local C&C Factory. But there had been rumblings of late that the factory might close and move out of state. With their military career secured, the boys would be able to fill in the gaps for their families if they lost those long-held jobs.

"Janey Marsden," called the announcer.

Janey Marsden was a particular bright spot. Not only had she earned the highest honors in the training program, but she'd also earned the highest honors in the whole class. Every soldier beamed as she gave the Valedictorian speech.

Teachers had welcomed the soldiers the first time they showed up at the school a year ago. When the soldiers had offered to take on their troubled kids, the administration had leaped at the offer to give the kids more attention.

Eight out of the eleven kids the soldiers had taken under their wing were now going into the military. That success rate had given some pause.

The next class was only six students. Word of mouth was how they had gotten those few new students. No teachers, guidance counselors, or principals were returning their calls for another visit.

The ceremony concluded, and Chase joined the others in congratulating the kids and their parents. Off to the side, he spotted the school's principal. He made his way over to the slight young man. Chase didn't miss the wince when Principal Miller caught sight of him in his peripheral eye.

"Principal Miller, a word if you have a second?"

"It's a big day," said Miller, not meeting Chase's eyes. "Lots of families to congratulate and students to say goodbye to."

"I understand that, but you also have a lot of students still here awaiting their future. As you saw, the JROTC program helped a lot of them forge a solid path for their futures."

"Yes, including one of our best and brightest. Did you know Janey Marsden was offered a full scholarship to three Ivy League schools?"

Yes, Chase did know that. And she'd decided to

use her bright mind in service to her country. He couldn't be more proud.

"But she's turned them all down to join the Army."

"I'm failing to see the problem," said Chase. "The military needs the best and brightest."

"Look, you can come after school to talk to the kids in detention. But coming into the classrooms again is just out of the question. Some of these kids have real potential."

"And the ones who get into trouble don't?"

The man sighed. "Look, I think the military is a viable path. But it shouldn't be the first road for some kids."

Chase's mouth opened, but only a choked sound came out. He was so shocked, he couldn't form words. He grit his teeth and clenched his fists as the man walked away.

A dull thud began just behind Chase's ear. He unclenched his fingers and rubbed at the spot. But it was useless. The migraine had dug in its tenterhooks.

Chase turned and faced the wall like a child in time out. He needed the solitude. After moments of deep breaths, he opened his eyes to find Dr. Patel beside him.

"You good?" the doctor asked. His wise eyes likely saw through Chase.

"I'm managing it."

Migraines were a common ailment. Not just to soldiers, but civilians alike. There was no immediate cure. Only management tactics. Quiet and darkness, sometimes a cold compress, was what worked for Chase.

"What brought that on?" asked Patel.

"Principal Miller thinks Janey's too good for the military. He won't let us speak to the full student body. He practically called us poachers. Can you believe that?"

Dr. Patel inhaled. "Once every family had someone in the military. That's not the case anymore. People today don't remember the honor it is to serve. That the military was the only viable path for some families."

"He can't bar us from the school," said Chase. "Can he?"

"No, but he can make it difficult. Want my advice?"

"Always."

Dr. Patel had been instrumental in Chase's healing. Chase had come to the ranch, mostly unscathed. His mind was intact, aside from the migraines. But he always enjoyed his talks with Patel and the advice the psychologist gave, but also the wise words of the man as pastor in the town's church. Chase rooted himself and prepared to take in Patel's wise gospel of scriptures and metaphors.

He enjoyed working out puzzles and riddles, which Patel often spoke in.

"My advice," began Patel, "is to go speak to the school board."

Well, that was uncharacteristically straightforward and logical.

CHAPTER FOUR

"With all the work I've done for the school board, how can you not be prepared to give me your flat out endorsement?"

Ginger tried to keep her voice light, but it trilled into incredulity. As a female politician, she knew she could never be perceived as shrill. That led to emotional and hysterical. She had to appear cool, calm, and collected at all times. Even when she wanted to stomp her foot at the sheer ridiculousness of some people.

"We can't endorse this far out from the election," said Dawn Weber, the school district's Assistant Superintendent.

Ginger squinted her eyes. Her hands jerked off the desk. She wanted to spout off the facts that the School Board had endorsed early before.

"You know you have my vote. But Senator

Norman Dean has a long history with the teacher's union."

"Dean hasn't kept a single one of his promises. I have a plan to-"

"Having a plan doesn't mean anything if you don't have any followers backing the plan."

"What's that supposed to mean?”

Dawn sighed. “Senator Dean has donors."

Ginger was staying away from the donor class. She didn't want to be beholden to anyone but her constituents. That's how government service should be.

"Money talks, Ginger. I don't make the rules.”

"I have money."

Ginger was running her campaign with her own money, money from a trust fund she swore she'd never touch. But it wasn't for her. It was for the people. At least that's how she justified it. And she hadn't put a dent in the fund.

Plus, she knew that money could say cruel things. She was one to know. She'd come from cruel money. She had plans to make it say nice things.

"I have small donors,” said Ginger. “Lots of parents."

"I know,” said Dawn. “I've seen your social media campaign. It's clever."

She'd done the campaign herself. Put her graphic design degree to good use. There was the Oh, Snap slogan playing off her first name. And the Sugar and Spice slogan playing off her surname and the family sugar business.

"But not a lot of people here are on social media outside of Facebook groups of their families," said Dawn.

Ginger's glossy Instagram and Snapchat ads had gone viral. But to the wrong demographics.

"The truth is, you're young, untried, and unmarried."

"What does my marital status have to do with anything?" Ginger said.

"Don't be naive, Ginger. You talk about commitment and compromise, and you have no proof that you're capable of either."

"That's just insane." Her voice went shrill.

Dawn leaned back. "I don't make the rules."

No, the patriarchy did.

"Your best bet is to get an endorsement from a high society member. Like your father."

Ginger had no intention of seeking out her father. Not after the stunt, he pulled with Honey. All her life, she'd given him chance after chance. But the man was who he was.

It was clear Ginger wasn't going to forge a path here with Dawn, so she took her leave from the office. Outside the door, a reporter lay in wait. It was a school board meeting tonight, which was big news here in this small town.

"Can I get a quote, Ms. Dumasse?"

Ginger opened her mouth to give a canned sound bite, but her voice was drowned out by a deeper tenor.

"It's about having a plan. But not only having a plan. It's about learning how to make a plan, implement it, and evaluate it."

Ginger turned to the resonating sound of sanity and blanched.

"That's what the military taught me," said Sergeant Colin Chase.

He stood in his uniform before the school board. It was the second time she'd seen him decked out in all his patriotic glory. She still had dried dribble on her chin from the first time.

"I come from a wealthy family, but none of that mattered in the service. The Army was truly the great equalizer. There, I learned the value of compromise and commitment. The Purple Heart Ranch's JROTC program has taught that to many kids in the community who didn't have a plan, who didn't know what was in the future for them, who had odds stacked against them because of their birth, or their race, or their economic status. But they can rise in the service."

"No one here disagrees with you, Sergeant," said one of the board members. The man looked haggard and bored.

For most of the school board, this wasn't their day job. Many members were eager to get home and kick their shoes off after a long day at work and an evening hearing teacher and parent grievances and demands. They did not appreciate long speeches. Ginger had learned that the hard way.

"What is it you are here for, Sergeant?"

Chase cleared his throat. When he spoke, his voice sounded even more deep and resonate. "I'm having trouble gaining access to local schools for recruitment efforts."

"What kind of problems?"

"Some faculty and students protest."

"That is their right. We can grant you access to the school premises, but you'll have to change their minds about the military."

Chase's jaw tensed. He nodded and stepped away from the podium. The moment he did, his eyes caught hers. They were always catching her. Probably because she was always staring at him when he was near.

He had made a good sales pitch. But it was a hard sell in a world where tech jobs were the wave of the future, and the military base pay was less than the minimum wage of most states. Chase needed to find a way to emphasize other benefits if he had any hope of getting his foot in the schools.

But that wasn't her problem.

As Chase turned away from the board, a large figure blocked him from Ginger's sight. Norman Dean had his hand out to Chase. Ginger saw Chase's hand hesitate, but in the end, he took the proffered hand and shook.

That was all she needed to hear and see. She and Colin Chase were truly on opposite sides of everything. Ginger turned from the doorway and headed to the elevator.

CHAPTER FIVE

Chase was used to giving orders. He was used to others following behind those orders or at least offering constructive feedback. So, when the school board dismissed his directive so easily, he balked.

He stood stunned for a moment, as though an explosive had gone off. The shock waves wore off quickly, though. He turned on his heel, but he knew he wouldn't be able to brush off the debris of this blowout. Before he could get out of the door, an icy palm clamped down on his shoulder.

"I think we may be able to help each other out, son."

Chase turned his head and met with Santa Claus. The man's body was a perfectly round ball in a straining white button-down. White tufts of hair protruded from his chin, his cheeks, and above his upper lip. But his head was bald. He wore a jolly smile, but it was his dark, beady eyes that told Chase this man only had access to the naughty list.

Chase could brush all the Bad Santa aside. There had been plenty of men promising sweets and delivering coal parading around his father's offices when he was a kid. What Chase couldn't abide was being called son. It was a power play. Even when his own father said it.

"Name's Norman Dean. I know your father."

Well, that explained the jolly old flashbacks. Mr. Dean stuck out his hand. Because Chase had been raised with manners, he accepted the cold shake.

"I'm running to keep my seat as state senator, which I've held for over two decades now."

So, this was Ginger's rival. The two couldn't be more opposite. Norman Dean was an older man promising candy cane dreams. While Ginger was a young woman and making plans to deal with the harsh realities of the day. Plans Chase didn't always agree with, but at least she was dealing with the truth of the matters.

"I can use an honorable man like you on my campaign," said Mr. Dean.

"As part of the military, we aim to stay out of politics, Senator Dean. As soldiers, we protect every citizen."

Dean threw back his head and laughed. It was a

ho-ho-ho that made the spine tingle in the wrong direction. "Everyone has a political agenda, son."

"Not me." Chase gave a curt nod and turned. "If you'll excuse me."

"You'll change your mind," Dean said to his back. "When you do, give me a call."

Chase couldn't make it out of the room fast enough. Down the hall, the elevator doors were closing. He called out for the occupant to hold the doors but got no response. He made it just in time before the metal cage closed, slipping one hand between the two sides and forcing the doors back open. When they opened, the last person he wanted to see stood inside the elevator.

But if Ginger Dumasse was the last person he wanted to see, why did his heart kick out a few extra beats? Why did his lips part like they were ready to take a sip or a bite of something? Why did his hands itch as though they needed to reach out and touch?

Ginger's eyes flashed up at him. Those lush lips pursed. That regal nose lifted into the air. That proud chin jutted out. She would've been adorable if not for being, well, her.

For a split second, Chase contemplated the stairs. Before the thought could become action, his feet were moving. The doors of the elevator closed behind them before his mind figured out that he and Ginger were alone together. The last time they had been alone together, he'd almost kissed her.

"Ms. Dumasse."

"Sergeant Chase."

They retreated to their own corners as the elevator began to move. The school board was housed in an old building. The elevator had likely been the first of its kind installed. It creaked along, groaning and moving slowly with old age. There were only three floors. The board meeting had been on the top. The elevator's pace was such that Chase could've walked down the stairs and back up all before the elevator made it to the second floor.

After another long groan of their cage and a rattling shake, Ginger reached out for the wall to brace herself.

Chase opened his mouth to offer comfort. And then promptly closed it. She'd reminded him enough that she was an independent woman. He was sure she didn't need his reassurance.

"Saw you getting cozy with Senator Dean back there." She took her hand off the wall and wrapped it around her torso.

"Jealous?"

Why did he like the idea that she was jealous of anything he might do. Maybe because it meant she cared. But that was ridiculous. They had a mutual dislike for each other.

Well, no, he didn't dislike her. He just disagreed with her. She wasn't a bad person. She wasn't even mean. She was just opinionated. Very opinionated, and she thought her opinions were right. She'd have made a great drill sergeant if she had a positive view of the military. Which she didn't.

"Jealous of what?" Ginger scoffed. "That he made you a bunch of promises to get your vote. Promises that he won't keep."

"Isn't that the way politics works?"

"Not my kind of politics. I'm a woman of my word."

Chase hadn't had any reason to test her word. But he believed her. Ginger Dumasse was fiercely protective of her sister. And he knew some of her background. What he particularly respected was that after her parents' divorce, Ginger had chosen to live with her mother in near poverty rather than cow to her wealthy father's demands.

"They're right about you needing a better portrayal for your cause," she said. "You need to focus on the aspects that matter to people today."

A better portrayal for his cause? What did that mean? Make military service shiny and glossy? Sell it?

That was ridiculous. He was offering these kids a way out, a plan, a chance. That was the sale right there. Here's your opportunity at a future and a way to do it honorably.

Chase tried to hold his tongue as the elevator creaked along down from the second to the first floor. The silence ate at him. Especially when he was in the right.

"Honor and service are what the military is about," said Chase.

"This generation is more into public service, travel, adventure." She'd uncrossed her arms as if her guard was down. She snapped her fingers as though a brilliant idea occurred to her. "Maybe if you framed it as a gap year."

Her face lit up. For a moment, Chase was taken with the sheer beauty of her. Bright blue eyes. Her soft blonde hair could've been the rays of the sun. Too bad there was a cloud on the horizon. She'd gotten her facts wrong.

"It wouldn't be a gap year," he said, raining on her parade. "Service is at least two years."

Ginger shrugged, crossing her arms back over her body. It was like the sun had set on what had been a beautiful day. She didn't say anymore. Which was a pity? Her idea hadn't been bad. She just hadn't had all the facts.

"I just don't think it's right that kids are taught the military is a last resort," he said. "All I was asking for in there was an equal shot."

"You and me both," she muttered.

The elevator lurched again. Ginger took another deep breath. They should be on the first floor by now, but the snail's pace had slowed further.

"You okay over there?" Chase asked.

Ginger's spine straightened. "Fine."

The metal box lurched again as if trying to decide whether to be the tortoise or the hare. The jerky indecision caused both occupants to lurch. Chase caught Ginger in his arms before she crashed into one side of the wall. The lights went out, and the elevator came to a stop.

Ginger whimpered, burying her head in his chest. Chase wasn't afraid. He'd been trapped in worse conditions during his time in service. So, why was his heart beating twenty klicks a minute?

CHAPTER SIX

The world was dark and still inside the confining space of the steel box. But while she was suspended in midair inside the elevator, Ginger didn't know the metallic taste of fear. Because the elevator wasn't the hard cage she was focused on. Her senses were wrapped up in the fact that she was inside of Sergeant Colin Chase's arms, and she didn't want to leave.

Ginger was fine with confined spaces. She had gone from living in the lap of luxury in a mansion with more rooms than she could count to a two-bedroom apartment on the wrong side of town without skipping a beat. She liked tight spaces. She did not, however, like being trapped in a space where she didn't want to be.

That wasn't the case here. Being inside of Chase's hold reminded her of that space under a warm blanket on a cold night when she'd pull the four corners of the sheet in, tucking them under her toes and fingers. During those cold nights, she'd always tunnel into the mattress and burrow into the warmest spot. The warmest spot of Chase was just right of the center of his chest, where his heartbeat was strongest.

For the first time in a long time, Ginger's knees went weak. Her fingers dug into Chase's shirt. And she couldn't remember why she didn't have one of these male creatures on hand on a regular basis? This one sure beat the feel of the patchwork quilt she'd gotten from the department store last winter.

"You're safe," Chase soothed. "I've got you."

He brushed his fingers across her brow, placing a strand of hair behind her ear. Ginger's entire body shivered at the brush of his calloused fingertips. She'd been in Chase's arms before, during another moment of weakness. Why was she always going weak around him?

You're safe. I've got you.

Her body melted into his strong chest. She had never heard those words from a man in her whole life. Definitely not from her father. Surely, not from the two boyfriends she'd had in high school and college. They'd both been clueless. She took better care of herself than any man, and that included her father.

But in this moment of darkness, stillness, and

warmth, Councilwoman Ginger Dumasse was happy to hand over the keys to her wellbeing to Sergeant Colin Chase. She knew with certainty that he could handle any situation he was thrust into.

The colors on his uniform became visible as the lights came back on. Now out of the darkness, those colors brought her to her senses. The sharp contrast between the dark colors of his uniform and the light colors of her business suit made her focus.

She and Chase were opposites. She disagreed with this man at every turn. Right?

But as he gazed down at her, Ginger couldn't remember a single thing she stood for. Was she for or against chin stubble, she wondered as she caught sight of Chase's five o clock shadow? What was her stance on kissing on the first date? Would she prefer a fall or summer wedding?

"I'll press the *help* button," he said.

His words snatched the edges of the warm blanket from her toes, letting the cold air hit her. She stepped back and out of his hold. "No, I've got it."

"You're wobbly," he said.

"I'm perfectly fine," she insisted.

Ginger stomped her foot down on the metal floor. But her right heel teetered on her pumps. The elevator lurched again, sending her back into Chase's arms.

She couldn't hide the wobbling or the teetering now. In fact, she was downright shaking. She was going to die in an elevator with Chase Collins. Senator Dean would run unopposed. Her issues, which she still couldn't quite remember, would never be brought to light. And the community she loved so dearly would continue to suffer without a clear vision and plan for the future.

But as she wobbled and teetered, she did it on firm ground with secure straps around her person. It was Chase. Her head was once again just off to the center of his chest.

"I'm going to get you out of here," said Chase.

His breathing was easy. His pulse steady. His demeanor one of total control, even though they were at the mercy of a rickety steel cage of death. But his heartbeat was racing too. It was the only thing that gave her any notice that he was human.

Meanwhile, Ginger was a quivering mess. Her limbs shook. She wasn't sure if she'd held back the cry that had lodged in her throat. And her heartbeat raced so hard she was concerned it might explode out of her chest.

No. This would not do at all for a woman who wanted to assume a leadership role. Ginger pushed off Chase and turned for the *help* button.

"I can get us out of here," she insisted as she depressed the button.

"You're not good at taking orders, are you?"

"You're not good at following behind a woman, are you?"

The red light above the *help* button turned on as if urging her to stop. She didn't. She never seemed to mind the boundaries when this man was involved.

"Your gender isn't an issue," said Chase. "I've had plenty of female superiors."

"So, what?" She cocked a hand on her hip. "You don't consider me a superior?"

Chase grinned. It was a devastating move. It turned his face from stern to handsome. "I think you're one of the smartest, most prepared persons that I've ever met."

Ginger came from a long line of pageant princesses. She'd rejected that lifestyle in her late teens. Hearing those words come out of Chase's mouth made her feel like she'd won the crown and the sash and the scepter. She wanted to preen under his compliments. But she sensed a *but* coming, so she tilted her head back as though to let any adornment slide off her head.

"But," continued Chase, "you can be too stubborn to do what's good for you. That's a mark against you."

Ginger pointed a finger at her chest. "*I'm* stubborn?"

Chase lifted a brow. The move made her dislike him more. The man had so much self-control that he could operate his facial features singly. It was unnatural and unfair.

"Because I offered to press a button?" she said.

"You didn't offer." He lowered his brow. "You demanded."

"Because I was in a better position."

"You were cowering in my arms."

"Cowering?" Both her brows rose to her hairline. "I do not cower."

"It's fine to be scared."

"I wasn't scared. I was startled." She pointed a finger at him. "And your heart was racing, too."

He didn't come back with an immediate retort. His throat worked like he was trying to gulp discreetly. Ha! So, soldier boy didn't have total control over his faculties. She'd gotten under his skin.

Ginger put her hands back on her hips. Her chest lifted in triumph. She wet her lips, preparing to go in for the kill.

Chase's nostrils flared. He let out a long, slow sigh as his gaze swept her body. Suddenly, Ginger's triumph felt like surrender.

He stepped toward her. Her fight or flight senses engaged. Her head told her to flee. Her heart told her to fly into his arms.

Now, it was Ginger who was trying to gulp discreetly. It didn't work. Chase's gaze latched onto her throat, and she would've killed for a glass of water.

He opened his mouth to speak. Before she was able to hear a single syllable, the ding of the door opening cut him off. They both turned to look out of the open doors.

They had arrived. They were on the ground floor. Outside the open doors stood the reporter who had badgered Ginger on the third floor.

Oh, no. If the newsman saw her and Chase together, they'd be paired again. The papers would label them a couple. Their names would be plastered all over the front page, linking them as involved with one another.

Which would be ... a bad thing. Right?

Luckily, the reporter's back was turned to them.

Which was a ... good thing. Right?

The last thing Ginger needed was to be linked to Sergeant Colin Chase for romantic or political reasons. And so she cleared her throat.

Fortunately, the reporter didn't turn around.

Ginger cleared her throat again. She coughed into her hands when the reporter continued staring down at his phone.

"Well, that's over," she said loudly.

"Yes," Chase agreed, his voice was too quiet to carry.

"Thank you for your service, Sergeant Chase."

At that announcement, the reporter hung up his phone. He slipped it in his pocket. And turned... toward the door.

Ginger let out a huff. The gust of air came loudly

from between her lips. But the reporter was already at the door.

She looked up to find Chase quirking that single brow at her again. Ginger wanted to growl. But she kept it in. Instead, she turned on her heel and promptly caught a snag in the decades' old carpet.

Her momentum propelled her forward, but her heel held her back. She was on her way to crashing down and let out a yelp of helplessness. Instead of meeting the dingy carpet that had captured her foot, she was caught by Chase's strong arms and brought once more to his strong chest.

And that's when the camera flash went off.

CHAPTER SEVEN

"Oh, oh, oh! Here's another one."

Ortega unwrapped the newspaper like it was an oversized Christmas present. But there was no box. It was the wrapping that had the soldier in a holiday tizzy.

On the one-page spread was yet another glossy headline with a photo of Ginger in Chase's embrace. The image wasn't snapped from last night. The picture was from Ortega and Honey's wedding when Chase and Ginger had been caught together in the barn.

Not that they had been doing anything wrong. Though, in that picture, Ginger was gazing in his eyes like she wanted to do something. In that stolen moment, Chase had been staring at her lips. It had been easy to do at that moment; she had been quiet.

She had also been soft and vulnerable. Even

after they'd been snapped by that photographer, and convention said they should break apart, Chase hadn't wanted to let her go. He'd felt the same way in the elevator last night when she'd been in his arms. She'd been even softer, quieter, with a touch more vulnerability. Her eyes had gone wide, her lips had parted, her nostrils had flared.

Or maybe that was just the way she looked when startled? They had been surprised by the cameraman at the wedding. The elevator getting stuck was also an unexpected occurrence. Maybe that was just her fight or flight responses he was seeing.

Why did he even care? He didn't want to kiss Ginger Dumasse. Did he?

"The headline reads the Soldier and the Senator." Corporal Brandon Lucas frowned at the thin sheet. "They didn't even get your rank right."

"I think they were going for alliteration," said Private Reece Cartwright. He was the youngest of their group, and the most well-read.

"Sergeant and Senator are alliterative," countered Lucas.

The four men stood in Ortega's small kitchen in his home on the ranch. The three men of Chase's unit all still lived on the ranch, at least for the time being. Brandon and his wife Reegan were rebuilding her family's home back in the heart of town. Reece and his wife Beth had learned not too long ago that they were expecting, so they were looking for a new home of their own in town. Mark's wife, Honey, was a former society miss. Chase caught sight of the young woman out the window with her hands in the mud, streaks of grass and grime were painted all over her shirt and pants. Honey loved the ranch and had no plans to return to high tea and ballrooms any time soon.

"It says she's only dating you to get her poll numbers up and to court the older voters who don't like her single status." Ortega frowned. "That's libel. Ginger is nothing like that."

Chase didn't say anything. Norman Dean had told him that an endorsement from a military man would lift his poll numbers. Chase wouldn't put it past Ginger. Politicians were all alike. His father had enough of them in his pocket for Chase to know.

But Ginger hadn't made Chase any offers. She hadn't tried to do any deals under the table with him. She hadn't even asked for his support. All she'd tried to do was convince him of her side of the issues. He didn't disagree with where she wanted to go, just how she planned to get there.

"What are you going to do about this?" Ortega demanded.

"Do?" asked Chase. "I'm not going to do anything."

"They printed lies," said Ortega, taking on his

brother-in-law role. "About both of you. We can't let this stand."

Ortega put the paper down and focused on Chase. His eyes went over his face, left to right and back again as though he were reading Chase.

"Unless there is something going on between you two," said Ortega.

"Wait?" Lucas turned his back on Chase and faced Ortega. "I thought there was something going on between them."

"Yeah, me too," said Cartwright, also giving Chase his back. "And that they were just keeping it quiet."

"Is that true?" asked Ortega.

At least he had the decency to face Chase as he inquired about his private business. The other two men turned back around, giving Chase their full attention.

Outside the windows, leaves were falling off trees. A few brown and red blades aimed at the windows. They hit the glass with soundless thuds and dropped to the ground.

"There's nothing going on between me and Ginger Dumasse."

The three men traded knowing looks. Before any of them could voice their unwanted opinions, the back door exploded open, and a small army stormed in.

Maggie Banks came in with a baby in her arms and three dogs at her feet. "Oh, good, there you are, Chase. I was hoping you would invite Ginger to Sunday dinner."

The three stooges standing off to the side each wore wide grins. They knew their job in this battle was done. Reinforcements had arrived.

"Why don't you ask her sister?" Chase said. "Or call her yourself."

"I figured you'd see her sooner." Maggie switched the baby to her other hip.

Behind him, Chase heard snickering from the peanut gallery. The dogs all looked up at him, panting and drooling as they waited for his response.

"Ginger and I aren't dating."

"Yeah, right." Maggie snorted. "But can you ask her anyway? And let her know she's always welcome at our table. She's practically family."

Chase opened his mouth to ... To what? There was no sense arguing with this bunch. Their minds were made up on this issue. It didn't matter that they were wrong.

"So, this is where the party is." Reegan came into the back door behind Maggie. "Oh, hey, Chase. Is Ginger coming to church this Sunday?"

"I don't know. We're not-"

"Make sure you guys pencil in couple's night out at Patel's restaurant, too."

Chase snapped his mouth shut. Why waste his breath?

"Welcome to the club." Lucas clapped Chase on his shoulder before going over and embracing his wife.

As plans for his life were being made, Chase escaped the madhouse through the front door. He made it all the way to the parking lot and into his truck without any more interruptions or invitations. The long drive back into town helped to clear his head. He loved his team. He loved the women on the ranch. But they had this mad idea that everyone should be in a relationship.

He wanted a family. Someday. But he had another passion to tend to first.

Thirty minutes later, Chase pulled into the recruitment center. It was tucked at the end of a shopping strip that featured a convenience store, a coin laundry, and a Chinese food takeout. Not the highest traffic. So, he was surprised to see someone waiting outside the door of the center.

When the man in shirt and tie saw Chase in his truck, he waved. So, it wasn't a mistake. He was waiting for Chase.

Chase climbed out of the vehicle and approached. As he got closer to the center's door, he heard a peculiar sound. It sounded like the phone was ringing inside the offices. It wouldn't be Ortega. The man had his cell phone number.

"You're Soldier Chase?" asked the man waiting in front of the door.

"Sergeant. Sergeant Chase."

"Right. I'm David Jacobs, the Assistant Principal at Charbury's Private Academy. We'd love for you to come and speak with our students."

"You would?"

"Yes."

"About the military?"

Mr. Jacobs waggled his head, neither up and down or left or right. "We're thrilled that Councilwoman Dumasse is taking an interest in the military."

"Well, I don't know if she is interested in the military."

"Her beau is an officer, so I have to assume she is. I'm hoping she might take an interest in a bill that deals with private school funding."

A bill? Private schools? Chase opened his mouth to correct the man, but the phone rang out again.

"Would you come in, Mr. Jacobs. I just need to get that."

Chase unlocked the door. He got to the phone before the call ended.

"Is this Sergeant Chase?" asked the caller. "The one dating Councilwoman Dumasse?"

Chase let out a long breath as he slumped into his chair. "How can I help you?"

"This is AgriCo, we're a lobby group for Montana

Farmers. I wonder if you might be interested in speaking at our annual meeting. Your girlfriend is invited too."

Chase bit his lip. He looked from the man in front of him to the phone receiver. He knew where both of these conversations were going. But just like with the issues with Ginger, just like with his friends back on the ranch, he might disagree with the tactics, but he didn't disagree with the end result. Perhaps he could walk this path on his terms.

"Well, do I have the right man or not?" said the man in the receiver. "Is this the sergeant dating the senatorial candidate?"

CHAPTER EIGHT

"Have you seen these polls?" Carla waved a stack of papers in front of her as she came into Ginger's office. "You're up amongst middle-aged women. And you're dominating college-educated women and career women. Not to mention, you've ticked up ten points with those in the military and military families."

"Hmmm." Nodded Ginger. She wasn't listening. She was too busy looking at the photograph on the society blog site.

It wasn't the image of her and Chase locked in an embrace in the barn back on the Purple Heart Ranch. No, that one was emblazoned in her mind. It was often the last thing she saw before she went to sleep each night ... and then dreamed of what would've happened if the cameras hadn't caught them at that moment.

Nope. That image wasn't in her mind now. A different series lit up her cerebral cortex. There was a series of pictures of Chase in the spread of the gossip rag.

Chase as a young man. Chase in a suit. Oh, she couldn't take her eyes off Chase in a suit; dark blue that perfectly complimented his dark hair. Not that Chase in his uniform wasn't everything. But the sergeant in that suit was more. So much more.

"I'm so glad you took my advice on this." Carla plopped down in the seat opposite Ginger's desk and kicked off her expensive heels.

"Hmmm," said Ginger. Chase's middle name was Jefferson. Colin Jefferson Chase. How presidential.

"Just a few more snapshots of you two together, and we'll overtake Dean in many of the key categories where you're trailing."

"What?" Ginger lifted her gaze from Chase's profile. She had to blink a couple of times to bring her best friend into focus. All she saw was the calculating gaze of her campaign manager.

"Chase. Bring him to the county fair. Let people see you on his arm. I'll need to get you a softer outfit, maybe pastels. And we'll leave your hair down for that fresh, girl-in-love look."

"In love?"

"You can pretend," said Carla. "Though I doubt you'll need to."

"What? Wait, no. This story is completely fake news. We're not dating."

"You're faking it." Carla flitted her fingers, waving the notion away. "I get it. Just fake your way into a few more photos and appearances."

"I'm not not faking it with Chase."

"So, it's the real deal. Fan-freaking-tastic. It's about time you got you some."

"I'm not getting anything." Ginger's cheeks heated. The blush spread across her shoulders. Luckily, she was wearing a blazer today. "You know what I'm trying to say. Chase and I aren't real dating. We aren't fake dating. We aren't anything."

Carla lifted a single eyebrow. Ginger growled. Maybe if she got Botox, she'd be able to pull off that singular feat.

"We just got stuck in the elevator," said Ginger. "It was a disaster. We couldn't even work together to get out. We are two of the most incompatible people on this planet. The man is insufferable."

"Insufferable? Okay, Lizzie Bennet."

"Don't start with me." Ginger pointed a finger at her friend. "I told you I wouldn't play the fake game with my social life or my political career. I have principles."

So, why had she tried to get that reporter's attention last night? Why had she felt a sense of accomplishment when she'd finally succeeded? Why had a rush of adrenaline gone through her when she saw the flash of his camera? Why hadn't she slept last night as she waited for the first mention of the news of herself and Chase?

Because she was attracted to Chase. Because she wanted to date a guy like that; strong and principled —even if he was wrong—with a chiseled jaw that she wanted to see crack into a smile.

"I know that look," said Carla, leaning across the desk. "You like him."

"I do not." Ginger crossed her arms over her chest. Was the AC on in her office? It was suddenly hot on this fall day. "We have nothing in common."

Except, despite the fact that they pointed toward different directions, they both wanted to ensure kids had options for their futures. He was a planner like her, which she had to admit was kinda hot. But ...

"We're on opposite ends of the political spectrum."

That was true. But they had both had similar upbringings where they came from wealth and forged a path on their own in spite of their family's money. And Chase was all for women in leadership. But ...

"The Chase angle is a non-starter. We need to stick to the plan. This media hoopla," which she had been instrumental in starting, "will die down." As long as she steered clear of being alone with him in barns and elevators. "I don't care if I see him again."

There was a knock at the door.

"Ginger, there's a Sergeant Chase here to see you."

And now she'd need to steer clear of her campaign office too? No way. This was her turf.

What was he doing here? He probably thought the headlines were her idea. He was likely about to storm in her office and accuse her of using him for her political gain.

Great.

Ginger tugged her lip into her mouth. And then stopped. She didn't want to ruin her lipstick. Maybe she should apply more? Had she applied mascara? She'd rushed out this morning and stuffed her makeup in her bag, intent on doing her face at the office. Well, she was at the office, and she didn't remember applying any foundation or mascara.

Oh, for the love of all things!

She caught sight of herself in the window's reflection. Her blouse was a bit wrinkled. There was a scuff on her heel. And she'd missed her manicure appointment the other day. Maybe she could ask him to come back later when she was more put together?

"Can I show him in?"

"Yes," said her traitorous friend.

Carla grinned at Ginger as she rose. Unlike Ginger, Carla was perfectly made up and manicured. Unfortunately, Ginger couldn't murder her couture'd bestie. They had guests.

Chase appeared in the doorway. Thankfully, he wasn't in a suit or uniform. He was in jeans and a T-shirt, but he looked like a million bucks. His eyes landed not on her but on her campaign manager. Chase offered Carla a smile, and Ginger saw red.

"Nice to meet you, Sergeant Chase. I'm Carla Holt, Councilwoman Dumasse's campaign manager."

"Nice to meet you, Mrs. Holt."

"It's Miss." Carla was still holding onto Chase's hand. "But you don't need to concern yourself with that."

Ginger was too concerned with Carla's claws still being wrapped around Chase's hands. Finally, Carla released her prey. Chase shoved his hand in his pocket, and Ginger felt an acute sense of loss.

"Ginger, you don't have any appointments all morning," Carla said with a wink. She walked toward the door with a little too much of a sway in her hips. The door closed behind her with a quiet snick.

Ginger was left with Chase. The man's presence took up the small space of her office. He didn't offer her a smile. Instead, his brown gaze scrutinized her.

"Listen," she said, "before you say anything, I just want you to know I had nothing to do with it."

"I know."

"The press can be salacious. They have to sell papers. So, they print ridiculous things."

"I understand."

Ginger stopped talking. She took a few tentative steps around her desk to come and face him. He didn't look upset. His brows were down in one line as he gazed at her. His expression was thoughtful, calm.

"You do?" she asked.

"Yes." He nodded. "It's ridiculous."

"Ridiculous?" It was a feat, but Ginger held herself perfectly still as the whiplash of his statement struck her across the face. "You mean you and me?"

It was almost imperceptible. She only saw it because she watched him so closely. Chase's gaze dipped to her lips, then back up to her eyes.

"But everyone believes we're together," he said. "No matter how ridiculous it is."

His gaze dipped to the papers on her desk. The ones that showed them in an embrace. And the ones that showed her rise in the polls.

"Looks like you're reaping the benefits of the ridiculousness," he said.

"Sergeant—"

"Call me Chase."

Those brown eyes slid back to hers. She felt like she was being bathed in warm chocolate. Sweet and velvet and warm.

"Chase." His name felt like a Hershey's Kiss on her tongue. She had to swallow the richness of it down before she could continue. "I want you to know that that's not how I run my campaign. It's not how I live my life. I don't use people to get ahead. I shoot straight, and I play fair."

He smiled at her. When he'd aimed that missive at Carla, Ginger had seen red. Now that the brown of his gaze was trained on her, she was ready to drop her principles.

"Can I take you to lunch, Ginger?"

"Lunch? Why?"

"Because it's not using if we both agree to it."

"*O*rder whatever you want. I'm buying."

Chase expected an argument. Instead, Ginger opened up the laminated menu and began to peruse it. Her silent acquiesce unnerved Chase.

"No argument over the bill?"

She looked up over the menu. As they always did, her blue eyes struck him like a bolt of heat straight into the chest. But it was the smile that unmanned him. He'd seen her smile, just not at him.

Blue was the hottest part of a fire. But the red of her lips, which should've been the cool part, rang a four-alarm fire in his mind. All of a sudden, Chase was unsure of the plan he'd come up with. It was very likely that he was about to get burned. Even more probable that he would like the singe.

"No argument," she said. "I believe a man should pay for a woman's meal."

"I took you for a feminist."

"I am." She set the menu down, folding the two halves neatly in front of her. "I believe in equal rights and equal pay. Other than that, I'm pretty traditional. Men hunt. Women gather. God made it that way. So, I have no arguments there."

Chase knew there was a *but* coming. He leaned forward in anticipation. Not that he wanted to argue with this woman. Far from it. He simply liked engaging with her, and currently, arguing was the only means with which they did that.

"But," Ginger continued, "mankind made money, not the Lord. Since we created it, women should get their equal share. Regardless of whether they have to work inside or outside of the home."

Interesting. But Chase didn't say so. The pile of things they were on the same side of was growing alarmingly tall. If they kept agreeing, what would they have to argue about? Then what reason would they have to be around each other? Their entire relationship was predicated on disagreeing with one another.

"Do you disagree?" she asked.

"No," he said. "A man should provide for a woman."

"Are you saying a woman can't provide for a man?"

"Not at all. But the partnership will be weaker if he doesn't."

"What if she's a better earner, and he decides to stay home with the kids?"

"That's admirable. Personally, I plan to provide for my family, come home in time enough to raise my children, and pamper my wife after she gets home from a long day of work."

"Lucky woman."

They stared at one another. Neither blinked. But this time, her gaze wasn't a challenge.

Did he note a hint of interest? Chase didn't dare blink as he tried to discern what was flickering in that cool blue gaze. The waiter's arrival broke the trance, and they both looked away at the same time.

"I'll have the tuna salad sandwich, extra onions," said Ginger as she handed over the menu. She turned back to Chase and added, "What? It's not like I'm going to kiss you."

Chase bit his lip to keep from chuckling. "I'll take an Italian sub, extra garlic, please."

The waiter went to the back with their odorous orders. Chase lifted his gaze back to Ginger. That note of interest was still there. He decided not to wait and just go for it.

"So, here's my proposal."

Her brows lifted. He probably shouldn't have used the word *proposal*. This was a fake arrangement, a convenient arrangement. It wouldn't lead to anything permanent. Definitely not her coming home to him at night to be pampered after he put the kids to bed.

"My suggestion," he said, "is that we don't correct the papers or anyone when they say we're together."

"But ... we're not together." Her voice was hesitant. The interest in her gaze was replaced with that touch of vulnerability.

"No," he agreed. "But no one believes us when we tell the truth."

Ginger rolled her eyes and nodded her head. Clearly, she had a peanut gallery of her own that she was dealing with if her campaign manager's behavior was any indication.

Chase continued on with his plan of attack. He'd thought this through at every angle, just like he would a battle plan. "So, we use it to our advantage."

"Our advantage?"

"You got a lift in the polls from being seen with a veteran."

She didn't nod. She didn't need to. They both knew how these things worked. He was gratified that she didn't try and orchestrate it.

"We're seen together at a few choice events," he continued. "I'll keep my mouth shut and smile adoringly at you."

Ginger's soft gaze turned to flint. "That won't be too hard for you?"

"What?" he grinned. "Smiling adoringly at you?"

"No, keeping your mouth shut."

He cracked a grin. Why had he thought this plan would be a hardship? Ginger Dumasse made every moment interesting.

"Why are you doing this again?" she asked.

"People are inviting me to speak at their events and organizations. That's all I want, a chance to make a case for joining the service. If I can just get people to hear me out, then maybe a few will actually listen, and I can change some young people's futures by bringing them into an organization that I believe in."

"This is fascinating." Ginger shook her head, her smile growing wider. But it wasn't a smile of joy. It looked annoyed. "For most of my political career—heck, for most of my life—I've been told I need to be on a man's arm to be taken seriously. Now, a man wants to use my arm so that he can be heard."

"So, you'll do it?" Chase asked.

"I have to." She shrugged. "Do you know how far ahead this will push the women's movement?"

Chase couldn't keep it in any longer. He threw back his head and laughed. After a second, Ginger joined him. Yes, she certainly made every moment interesting. Especially when she turned traditional conventions on their nose.

Soon, the laughter died down, and her shoulders drooped. "But there's one problem. You don't agree with anything I stand for."

"That's not true," he said.

"Oh, really? I believe education should be a kid's highest priority after graduation."

"I agree. I just believe education can be had in college, in trade, and even in the military."

She pursed her lips. Chase tried not to think about how they might taste. Where was that tuna sandwich?

"There's just one more issue we should discuss," she said. Her features went grave. "I believe that soccer is a far superior sport than football."

Chase picked up his napkin and threw it down on the table. "This relationship is over."

Ginger giggled. It was a delightful sound. A sound he could easily get used to.

The waiter brought out their smelly food, and they dug in. Unfortunately, the smell of fish and onions and garlic did nothing to tamp down his desire. He wasn't sure anything could stop his growing interest in this woman.

"I was serious about soccer, you know."

CHAPTER TEN

The screams of children and crank of wheels filled Ginger's ears. She turned her nose away from the saccharine smell of the cotton candy and funnel cakes only to be confronted with the greasy smell of fried meat, fried desserts, and was that a fried beverage? It was the county fair, and it was part of her duty as a candidate to attend.

She'd posed for pictures with her constituents. Shc'd shaken hands with the union leaders. She'd held screaming, smelly babies. It was all par for the course.

"Smile," demanded Carla.

"I am smiling," Ginger insisted.

"Smile for real. What's on your face looks tired and fake."

Because she was tired and fake. Ginger wanted nothing more than to kick off her heels, toss off this skirt, and kick her feet up on her couch for the rest of the evening.

And eat. Sheesh, did she want to eat.

Her stomach growled. Loudly. Chase looked over at her with concern on his normally stern brow.

He was keeping up his end of the bargain by being her escort today. He hadn't said much after joining them at her campaign headquarters and riding over. He'd been a silent observer as she'd done the rounds. All the while, she felt his judging eyes. Why had she thought it was a good idea to put on this fake dating farce?

"Here," Chase said.

He presented her with a corn dog on a stick. It was golden brown and perfect. The scent of buttery goodness nearly made Ginger faint. She turned away before she had a moment of weakness.

"I can't eat that," she said.

"Don't tell me you're on a diet," he said. "I saw you put away a carb-loaded sandwich the other day."

"You did what?" said Carla.

Ginger shook her head like a child caught with their hand in the cookie jar. "It was whole wheat bread and low-fat mayo."

That didn't stop Carla's huffing. She insisted Ginger had to always look camera ready. Carbs put on pounds for the camera.

"She can't be seen eating," Carla said to Chase.

"She can't risk being photographed. There are press and smartphones everywhere."

Chase turned to Ginger, corndog still in hand. "So?"

It took Ginger a second to take her eyes off the heaven on a stick and look at the man. "I risk looking very suggestive eating, well, that."

Chase looked at the meat on a stick. He wrapped his hand around the breaded hotdog and pulled it from the stick. "I can break it into pieces for you."

Though tempting as the idea was to have him handle her food and feed her, Ginger still had to decline. "I risk looking like a cavewoman taking a bite."

Chase held the two halves of the corndog in each hand. Now that the seal of the bread was broken, the buttery scent went straight to Ginger's head.

"So you starve?" he asked.

Ginger swallowed down her hunger. For the corn dog, as well as for the man trying to provide her with the sustenance she so desperately needed. Looking like she was in command was all part of the plan.

"I want to win," she said. More to herself than to him. And the corndog.

"Can you drink?" Chase asked.

"Alcohol? No, it would look like I'm a lush."

"I meant a milkshake. Fruit, milk, sugar. Unless sipping from a straw is uncomely."

Chase took the plastic container he'd placed

between his arm and presented it to her. Ginger eyed the beverage. Again her stomach grumbled. She was about to give in. But it was showtime.

"Councilwoman Dumasse?"

She gave one last look at the shake and, by sheer force of will, turned to face the onslaught of curious voters. "Please, call me Ginger."

"Ginger, what's your position on upgrading farms to meet with today's demands?"

Ginger nodded sympathetically as she listened. She had a plan for that. "The world is changing. The way we receive food is different with delivery services. The way we grow food is changing, as well. Farms are becoming more and more technology-based. But that shouldn't scare those of us that work in fields."

She caught Carla's eye. Carla didn't look happy. The campaign manager didn't need to tell her. Ginger was stating too many facts and statistics. People wanted a story. Votes were emotional.

"I should know, I grew up on a farm. Sure, it was sprawling acres with a mansion. But I paid attention to what was going on in the fields. I understand what a hard day's work looks like. I also know that, increasingly, young people aren't going into farming. Machines can take some of the stress off the farming operations. But we'll need to invest in agricultural technology so that farms can thrive. I have a plan for that."

The man nodded, seeming impressed.

"What about healthcare?" said a woman off to the right. "My premiums are going up."

"I understand that, too. As many of you know, I was born with a silver spoon in my mouth. But that didn't last my whole life. My mother became sick, and we didn't always have the money to put food on the table and pay for her medicines. The state came to our aide, allowing us to keep our doctor and not pay exorbitant fees. I watched how they did that. I have a plan on how we can expand that program for all."

"That sounds all well and good," said another voter in the front of the crowd. "But taxes are rising, and jobs are few. What jobs there are available are computer-based. I don't have the skills to compete."

"That's where my education plan comes into play. I know many of our youth are leaving for the bigger cities. That's why we need to invest in job training for the young and old. These problems aren't insurmountable. Not when we focus on our commonalities and build from there. We are a community. We have lived together and thrived for hundreds of years because we hold true to the first tenet of American democracy, and that is an opportunity for all. That is the core of my being. That is who I am. That is what I have to offer you."

Heads nodded. There were murmurs of assent.

Ginger was most gratified to see Chase watching her thoughtfully with a small smile on his face.

"That works well for civilians," called out someone from the back. "But what about veterans?"

Ginger turned to the newcomer. She opened her mouth, but nothing came out. Her mind reeled.

Veterans? She didn't have any notes or plans for veterans.

"There are problems with vet unemployment, housing, and mental healthcare," the man continued. "Do you have a plan for that, councilwoman?"

"I ... um ..." She didn't.

"I assume since you're now involved with a veteran," the man said, "you've at least thought about these issues."

Ginger looked to Chase and gulped. His features were impassive. He wasn't going to come to her rescue. This wasn't part of their deal.

But Chase stepped up, putting his hand at the small of her back. He gave her an encouraging smile as he did so. It bordered on affection.

For a moment, she forgot that they were in a crowd. She simply gazed into the eyes of a strong man, one who had never once cowed when she stepped up to take the lead or state her plan. Every time she pushed or prodded Sergeant Colin Chase, he held firm, or he pushed back. Now, he turned to the newcomer and spoke for her.

"As a veteran, I know that the problems we face are similar to those of everyday civilians. Many of Councilwoman Dumasse's plans will work for those in my situation. She has spent time at the Purple Heart Ranch listening to the issues today's soldiers face. But as you know, she is a thoughtful woman who likes to see the problem from all sides. She'll be presenting a full plan soon."

Chase gazed down at her. This time, affection was clear in his brown eyes. The silence lingered. Ginger knew she should say something, but her tongue was tied. Her stomach grumbled again, but not from physical hunger this time.

"Now, if you'll excuse us. The councilwoman and I have a lunch date."

CHAPTER ELEVEN

Chase broke the corn dog into four, even bites. Then, using a fork, he dunked the fried morsel into ketchup. He glanced up at Ginger before dunking it into the mustard as well. When she didn't object to the pairing, his own mouth watered. He was hungry, but not for the breaded hot dog.

Ginger eyed each of his movements greedily. He caught a flash of white teeth as she bit at her bottom lip. Then a sliver of pink tongue as she wet her upper lip.

"Open wide," he said.

Chase lifted the fork. In went the food. Her lips encircled the tines of the fork, lingering. Chase wished he'd used his fingers.

"Mmmm," she mumbled around a mouthful. "That is heaven right there."

He watched her chew, unable to take his eyes off her. They were in his car, having ditched her detail and the crowd of voters eager to pester her with more questions. Chase had her all to himself.

They weren't secluded in a barn this time. They didn't have the privacy of a stuck elevator. Still, he shielded her body from prying eyes as he fed her another bite of food. It wasn't that he cared about any prying eyes. He was simply enjoying having her all to himself.

Beyond that, Chase was thrilled that Ginger wasn't on a diet. Her figure was perfect. Too perfect if you asked him. If Ginger Dumasse had a flaw, it might help him to stop sneaking glances at her.

She slipped her shoes off with the third bite and turned her body fully to him. Her lips opened before he commanded, anticipating the last bite.

"Is that all?" she asked after swallowing the fourth piece down.

Her lips pressed together in a pout. Her perfectly arched brows slumped. Her fingers clenched into tiny fists.

Now, Chase was the one biting his tongue. She was adorable, like a disgruntled kitten. Man, if he didn't want to pet her and make her mewl.

Instead, he said, "I can get you another one."

Ginger twisted her lips in thought. She eyed the dollop of ketchup still on the fork tine. Chase put the utensil down. Neither of them needed to have that happen.

"No," she said finally. "That was enough."

"Are you ready to go in?" he asked.

"I am if you are."

Chase looked across the parking lot toward the private school. Charbury Private Academy, the pristine sign read. It could have been a replica of the private school he'd gone to as a kid.

No students lingered outside the front door before the bell. There were no school buses lined up as all of the kids had their own cars or drivers. Nor were there any flyers announcing bake sales or school fundraisers. There was no need. Tuition, endowments, and donations likely more than covered everything.

"It's been years since I've been in there," said Ginger. "I was glad to leave it."

"You went to public school?"

She nodded but didn't elaborate.

Chase's spidey senses tingled. It was the feeling he got in the desert when all was too quiet. He'd learned to listen to that sense. It was a harbinger that there was something else out there. The tingling sensation went to his belly when he realized what had to lay behind her silence.

"Your father wouldn't keep paying for you to go here after your parents' divorce?"

Ginger shrugged, but her gaze wasn't on him. It

was out the window at the school. "I didn't want to go here. I never felt like I fit in with these kids. They didn't have any ambitions other than climbing the social ladder."

Chase understood that. It was the exact make up of his private school and his parents' social club. But he hadn't had a choice in changing schools. He would've made that choice if he could. By the way her nose turned up as she looked at the school, Chase got the sense that Ginger didn't regret having the choice thrust upon her.

Once again, he was stunned by how much they had in common. Maybe they could be friends after this?

"Community activist, councilwoman, and now state senatorial candidate." Chase ticked Ginger's accomplishments off on his fingers. "Seems like you've climbed pretty high up the social ladder."

She snorted. It was completely unladylike and entirely adorable. "Not if you ask my father. He couldn't be more disappointed in me."

That was a surprise to Chase. From what he knew of Henry Dumasse, the man coveted every advantage he could get. He'd even tried to marry off his youngest daughter for a profit.

"I take it, you two are on different sides of the issues?" asked Chase.

"Hardly. The side my father is on is the one that's the greenest." Ginger rubbed her index and thumb together in the universal sign for money. "He realized a long time ago that he couldn't buy me, and he's never forgiven me for it."

There went yet another tick in their similarity column.

"My father shares the same disappointment in me," said Chase. "He wanted me to join the family business. Instead, I joined the Army."

"Two community servants. What awful children we are."

Chase chuckled.

"I only accept small donations in my campaign. Absolutely no corporate sponsors. I pay my staff from my trust fund. I figure with all the wheeling and dealing my father's done that have hurt people in this community, it's the least I can do. I've barely put a dent in the monies, though."

"I used the inheritance my grandfather left me to secure the lease on the recruitment center."

Ginger took in a dramatic gasp and covered her mouth with her hand. "Why, Sergeant Chase, you naughty soldier. You used private funds to pay for a government enterprise?"

"They're still digging through the red tape. Meanwhile, I've helped a dozen men and women find a viable future for themselves and their families."

She gazed at him in silence for a long moment.

Chase held her gaze until his curiosity got the

better of him. "What?"

Ginger shrugged one shoulder. "You're a better man than I imagined you to be."

Chase mimicked her movement, shrugging one of his shoulders. "You're okay, yourself."

She balled her fist and punched him in the still raised shoulder. Chase pretended to fall into the door from the impact of her assault. She had moved him, but more on the inside than the outside.

"Well, let's get this over with," she said, slipping her shoes back on. "I'm sure you want to finish up your obligation to me so you can get back to your real life."

"Yeah." Chase watched as her pink toes slipped into the high heels, disappearing from his sight. "Yes, you're right. No, wait. I'll get the door."

"Chase, I can open my own door."

"Ginger, it's my car door. I always open it for ladies."

Her hand rested on the handle. "You have a lot of ladies in this car?"

"No."

He held her gaze. The vein at her neck jump. Her throat worked as she swallowed. He had to stop wondering how the skin at the column of her throat tasted. He had to stop wanting to kiss her. They might have things in common, but they were still all wrong for each other.

Ginger released the door handle. She sat back in

her seat with her hands folded primly on her lap. It took Chase a moment before his legs decided to work, and he could get out of the car.

She waited in her seat until he came around and handed her out. She hesitated before putting her hand in his offered one. But in the end, she relented and took his hand.

Big mistake.

A spark zinged up his arm. By the small gasp, he knew she'd felt it too. Chase rubbed her knuckles before releasing her hand. He wasn't sure if the move had been to comfort her or himself?

Assistant Principal Jacobs came out to the front office to greet them. "Sergeant Chase and Councilwoman Dumasse. Such a pleasure. Come in, the kids are waiting."

They started forward, but Jacobs wrapped a hand around Ginger's other arm and tugged.

"Councilwoman, while the Sergeant is talking with the students, I was hoping to tug your ear on a pressing matter."

Ginger's features shifted from relaxed to tense. The light that had been in her eye when she'd eaten the corndog dimmed. The smile she plastered on was fake and weary.

"I'm sorry, Mr. Jacobs," said Chase, wrapping an arm around Ginger, which broke Jacob's hold on her. "But Ms. Dumasse is here at my pleasure, not in any official capacity other than my girlfriend."

Chase felt the intake of breath as Ginger's shoulders straightened. He also felt a little kick to his gut once that single word left his lips. *Girlfriend.*

Not that it was true. But only they needed to know that. In any case, the ploy worked. Jacobs reluctantly let go of Ginger's arm, and they all proceeded down the hall.

Inside, Chase was confronted with a couple dozen kids in starched blue and white uniforms. The smell of trust funds mingled with a strong hint of entitlement. At least none held protest signs against the military. It was a good start.

"First, I want to thank you all for coming out to listen to me today. My name is Sergeant Chase. I served with the United States Army for six years. They were the best years of my life. I learned leadership, made lifelong friends, and was able to serve my country. I believe that the military is a viable career path, especially for bright minds like yours."

A hand went up. Chase pointed to a young man with gelled hair pushed back with Aviator sunglasses.

"I wanted to be a pilot when I was a kid, but I got into Harvard. No way are my parents going to let me give that up."

And here is where the problems started.

"You could think of it as a gap year."

That idea hadn't come from Chase. Ginger stepped up beside him. All heads swiveled to her.

"The minimum commitment to the military is two years." She turned to Chase for confirmation. After he nodded, she continued. "And I think you can serve on the weekends, once a month?"

"That's right," said Chase. "In the Reserves."

"I was thinking of joining the Peace Corps," said another student, a young woman this time.

"The Peace Corps is a great option," said Ginger. "But in the military, you would serve your flag, your home country."

"My parents want me to take a gap year," said a kid in a wrinkled shirt that was one size too small and a few scuffs at the knees of his pants.

"Do it while serving your country," said Chase. "You get to travel in the service. You'll be in the best shape of your life, too. There's adventure and public service. What more could you ask for?"

It looked as though a handful of the kids were actually considering it. Chase looked over to the woman standing beside him. She didn't know it, but this was a win. And he wouldn't have thought of any of those spins without her.

"I have a question, Sergeant," said the wrinkled shirt kid. "How's the food?"

And now he was back to square one. But at least he still had their attention.

"You guys make such a cute couple." Ginger didn't respond to Eva Lopez's query. She didn't want to be rude, but she didn't know the woman well enough to answer such a personal question. The two women had gone to high school together, but they hadn't run in the same circles.

Ginger had been active in clubs, but Eva never stayed after school. She'd had too many responsibilities. First, her sick parents, and then her two younger siblings to take care of. Now, Eva was nearing the completion of a college degree.

She still had her two siblings to care for, but she also had a husband. Eva—well, she supposed she was Eva DeMonti now—had married one of the soldiers who came to convalesce on the Purple Heart Ranch. Fran DeMonti had come to Montana with shrapnel in his heart. But when he met Eva, a miracle happened. The shards that could've pierced his heart moved aside to allow love in his life.

It was an amazing love story. One for the books, for sure. But Ginger didn't have time to read romance novels. She was too busy solving the world's real problems.

So, she pretended not to hear Eva's statement about her and Chase because Ginger knew there was a hidden question mark in there. A question mark that Ginger wasn't sure of the answer to.

Chase had called her his girlfriend back at the private school. But it had been part of the act. Hadn't it?

What hadn't been an act was the way her heart had flipped. The way her fingernails had dug into her palms with want. The way her body had melted and molded into Chase's as he'd put his arm around her.

"I knew there was something between them after that dinner," Maggie Banks was saying.

Ginger knew Maggie from high school, as well. Maggie had mostly kept to herself back then. Or she'd engaged whatever animal was about. Even now, the veterinarian had two dogs at her feet and a beautiful baby bouncing on her lap. Across the table, Maggie's husband, Dylan, sipped his sweet tea while gazing adoringly at his family.

Eva's husband Fran told knock-knock jokes with

her little brother while her little sister rested against Fran's healed chest.

Reece Cartwright and his wife Beth, who was the daughter of the town's pastor, held their own private conversation while his hand rested on her growing belly. Beside them, Reece's twin sister Reegan laughed at something her husband, Brandon Lucas, said.

Ginger was surrounded by happy brides and adoring husbands. The group included her newlywed sister. Mark Ortega hung on Honey's every word as she went on and on about the little projects she was taking up around the ranch. Ginger still couldn't believe that her sister, who had never gotten a single speck of dirt on her her entire life, had happily taken to ranch life like she'd been born to it.

"Chase is the last of his team that's single, you know?"

Oh, Ginger knew all right. She was made aware of that little fact any and every time she came and visited the ranch these past three months. Also, the hint was dropped each time she was in town and ran into one of the Purple Heart Brides as the townsfolk liked to call the women who lived on the ranch.

"I was sure you two would get together before his three months were up," Maggie was saying.

Ginger also knew all about the zoning issue that said anyone who lived on the ranch had to be married. The red tape read that soldiers only had three months to live in the housing on the ranch, or they had to get out. As a city representative, Ginger knew the clause could be easily fought and defeated in a court of law. But no one from the ranch had launched a complaint. Instead, they all complied.

Chase's other team members had all gotten married within the window. First Brandon and Reegan. Then Reece and Beth. And last month her sister had walked down the aisle with Mark. But Chase had stayed single the whole time. In fact, he'd moved off the ranch right at the three-month mark.

"I lost a bet because of you two," said Eva.

"The new bet is how long it'll take you two to get engaged," Reegan chimed in. "My money is on a month."

"I've got a week," said Maggie.

This was insane. Ginger had to come clean. Even though these women were pains in the neck about her relationship status, she did actually want to be friends with them. She wanted to belong in this tight-knit community that had embraced her sister. She missed having a family looking out for her.

And so she took a deep breath and let the truth out. "Guys, it's not real. It's fake."

Instead of having gazes narrowing at her in anger; rather than chins raising high in indignation; every woman's eyes went wide with joy.

"I'm changing my bet," said Maggie. "I give it a few days."

"I give it until the weekend," said Eva.

Bewildered, Ginger turned to her sister.

Honey shrugged. "Apparently, that's how it all begins. If you pretend to date or masquerade as a couple, the real thing follows."

Ginger knew Honey had done that with Mark during her debutante ball. Within a week, the two were in love and engaged. She'd heard a little about Maggie and Dylan's story where he'd proposed to save the ranch, and she'd said *I do* to save her animals. She knew Brandon had proposed to Reegan after her house had burned down. And Reece had believed he was already engaged to Beth when he'd experienced temporary amnesia.

Wow, this ranch was a haven for cheap romance novels.

Well, it wasn't happening to her and Chase. They weren't compatible. Even though he'd come to her rescue earlier, and she'd come to his. Even though his hand at the small of her back was the best thing she'd felt in a long time.

She felt it again now. A warm weight settling right between her shoulder blades. If she weren't sitting upright, Ginger would've sunk down into the cushion of that palm.

"Had enough?" Chase said into her ear.

She turned to find him grinning at her. The look

in his gaze was knowing, as though he'd been privy to a similar conversation with the guys.

"You want to get out of here?" he asked.

"Yes."

Ginger threw down her white napkin, signaling her surrender to the crazy conversation and betting still going on around her. As she headed to the door, there was the distinct sound of kissing noises. But when they turned, everyone at the table looked away innocently.

CHAPTER THIRTEEN

Chase couldn't keep his hands to himself. They'd rested on Ginger's shoulder blades as they walked out of the ranch's dining hall. He'd toyed with a strand of her hair as they made their way down the stairs. His fingers had brushed her ear lobe as they crossed the fields. She'd shuddered, but he'd been the one to get a shock.

All throughout dinner, he hadn't been able to take his eyes off her. Not for long anyway. He'd lost threads of conversations as he spoke with the other males around him. He answered in monosyllabic words when asked his opinion.

Each time he was able to tear his gaze from Ginger and back to his dinner companions, the men all wore goofy grins. At one point, Reed Cannon simply called him out.

"We're obviously not holding your attention," the Specialist had said. "Go talk to her. Sooner rather than later so I can win this bet."

"What bet?" Chase had demanded.

"Doesn't matter," chimed in Sean Jeffries with a rare smile on his scarred face. "Just get a move on before the weekend."

Something was afoot, but Chase couldn't spare a care. He was more than happy to leave the guys and move in on his true target. Ginger Dumasse had gotten under his skin. Not just under his skin. In his very fingertips. In the palm of his hand, which he now rested at the small of her back. She'd gotten into his mind through his nostrils, which flared to take in more of her spiced-sugar scent.

"That roast at dinner was really great," she said as they walked the graveled path.

"Yup," Chase agreed. "Tender and sweet."

"There was a bit of toughness to it."

"Just a bit around the edges," he agreed. "But it was well done in the center, where it counts."

"You think?"

Ginger stopped walking and turned to face him. Her eyes were bright stars in the moonlight. Her parted lips glistened, begging to be kissed.

What were they talking about again?

Chase took a deep breath to try and clear his head. He let the air out slowly. Tilting his head up, he looked to the sky.

Nope, those stars had nothing on the woman before him. Their shine was dim compared to the light within her. The light shining bright, warming him from the outside in. How had he ever thought her rigid?

"You wanna go for a ride?" he asked.

"You're ready to take me back home?" The disappointment in her town was clear in the darkness.

"No." Being parted from her was the last thing he wanted right now. "Not a car ride, a horseback ride."

"Now?"

Chase tugged Ginger along to the stables. The strong smell of horse manure brought some sense back to him. But not enough to turn back around.

He wasn't entirely sure what he was doing here, alone in the dark with this woman. He simply knew he didn't want to be anywhere else.

He lifted a saddle from the wall and opened one of the horse's stalls. "You know how to ride?"

Ginger grabbed hold of the straps and began buckling them. "Of course, I know how to ride. I'm from Montana."

Of course, she knew how to ride. She could probably run this ranch single-handedly. Was there anything this woman couldn't do? Nothing she couldn't plan for?

"Do *you* know how to ride, city boy?" she chided.

"I guess you're about to see."

Chase swung himself up on the horse. Then he extended his hand down to her. Ginger took it with a smile and saddled up behind him.

Chase knew it was a mistake the moment her arms wrapped around his waist. He recognized the miscalculation when her front pressed into his back. He sensed his misjudgment as her breath tickled the bottom of his earlobe. He may have made a mistake, but he knew this underestimation would pay out in huge gains.

And so he didn't back down. He didn't stop and step down from the horse that was ready to carry them into the night. He didn't turn around and admit to this error. He no longer wanted to run from what was clearly between them. With a slap to the horse's hide, they took off into the night.

The ranch by moonlight was a vision. The tall trees resembled fluffy clouds touching the sky. The stars were pinpricks in a dark blue comforter. Along with the moon, those pricks of light provided ample illumination to guide them along the path.

When he'd lived here, Chase had often gone riding alone at night. There was a peace in galloping over the green fields in the dark of night. With Ginger resting her chin on his shoulder, he felt like he could conquer the world.

They didn't speak. They didn't need to. He felt her every move; the brush of her fingers, the twitch of her thigh.

He was completely tuned into this woman. Probably had always been since the first time they'd argued with one another. How could he disagree with someone, but be in complete accord at the same time?

He knew how. Their differences didn't separate them. Their differences, and the stark boundary lines between them, simply outlined more clearly who they were.

The horse slowed to a canter as they headed back to the stalls. Chase dismounted first. Then he reached up to hand her down.

Ginger wasn't a slight girl. She was a healthy woman. He brought her body to his to brace her weight. Soft curves met hard muscle. They both gulped at the intimate contact as she slid down his body.

Chase watched intently as she slid down his chest, coming closer and closer. When her lips were just a couple of inches away, he knew that he would kiss her. He knew it was inevitable, had been since she'd given him his first tongue lashing over higher education versus military service.

Well, now she was about to learn something new. And he would be the one providing the service. His lips were less than an inch when it happened.

The pain was sudden and acute. He gripped Ginger to him instead of grabbing at his aching skull. It didn't matter. The stabbing migraine turned the dark night completely black.

Before he became completely incapacitated, Chase set Ginger on her feet and turned away to deal with the torment.

CHAPTER FOURTEEN

Chase was a big guy; a big, healthy, powerful guy. So, to watch his body convulse in pain was a shock to Ginger's system.

For the first time in a long time, she didn't know what to do. No steps formed in her mind. No process or procedure became clear. The only thing she knew she wanted to do was to make whatever was hurting him stop.

Chase's hands, those same palms that had spread warmth through her, cradled his head. Ginger turned her focus there. She put her hands over his. Her fingers aligned with his as he pressed against his temples.

She didn't know if it was enough. But it seemed to comfort him. His ragged breaths slowed. He stopped panting and began to take full, slow, deep breaths.

That was a start. But he still didn't pull his hands away. His brow was still crinkled in agony.

Was this a PTSD episode? She knew that many soldiers, more than were reported, re-experienced the trauma they saw and lived through when they came back into civilian life. Was Chase having a flashback? Was he remembering something horrible from his time in a combat zone?

Part of her brain flared a red warning sign. Ginger realized she should probably step back from him. She should put a safe distance between herself and him until she had more information as to what was happening. What if he didn't recognize her and lashed out at her?

No sooner than the thought rang in her mind did she dismiss it. This was Chase. Though he was big and often stern, every bone, every muscle in his body had shown her nothing but gentleness. Even when he disagreed with her, his tone had never been harsh.

He'd even placed her away from him when the episode began. He'd been thinking of her care and comfort even as he was experiencing pain. For that, but also for so much more, she would not leave him, whatever the consequences.

His hands still covered his face, like he was hiding from her. Ginger slid her fingers in between Chase's fingers to press directly against his skin. She knew she'd done the right thing when he sighed against her palm.

Soon, he let her have his head. His hands fell away, leaving only hers. Ginger worked hard to earn the trust he'd just given her. She kneaded in tight circles. Then in smaller circles.

The plan was working. Chase kept his eyes closed. His breath steadied, going from ragged gulps to easy inhales and even exhales.

Ginger didn't speak as she cared for him. She somehow knew that sound would not be welcomed. She waited for him to initiate conversation.

He didn't. He remained quiet, reverent almost as she rubbed at his sore spots.

At some point in her maneuvering, her fingers moved away from his temples. They traced his jawline. She felt the prickly stubble there that had begun around five o'clock this evening.

As she came closer to his mouth, Chase's chin lifted. His eyes opened to reveal the dark pools of brown. And, finally, his lips moved.

"I have a headache," he said.

"Isn't that supposed to be my line." She grinned.

Chase didn't return her smile. He didn't lean in to taste her lips. His head was still in her hands. But, slowly, he was taking the weight of it from her.

"This is for the best," he said as he leaned back.

What did that mean? What was for the best?

"I'll give you a ride home," he said.

"I drove," she said.

"I'll walk you to your car, then."

The softness was gone from his voice. She could hear the residual pain laced in his tone. Was he pulling the guy thing? She'd seen him vulnerable, and now he had to macho up? Was that what was going on?

As if she hadn't just spent the last ten minutes tending to him, giving him comfort, letting him know that she wouldn't hurt him, that she could, in fact, help take away the pain. All that, and he was now shutting her out. Well, screw that, and the horse he came in on!

"Don't bother," she said. "I can do it myself."

Ginger whirled around. She pumped her legs hard as she made her way back up the path. She couldn't get to her car and away from Sergeant Chase fast enough.

The moment she heard his footsteps, she whirled around to face him. "You know, I don't need you to be my knight in shining armor."

"I wasn't trying to be," he said.

"Yet, the moment you show a sign of weakness, you run."

"I didn't run. I was on my knees with my head in your hands."

"And what? That scared you? Being vulnerable in front of a woman."

"I'm not scared."

"Oh, yeah?" She squared off against him and poked him in the chest. "Then why are you sending me away? Why put distance between us if you're not scared?"

"Because I don't want this." His voice was raised as he motioned his hands between the two of them.

Ginger reared back as if he'd slapped her. His words certainly did. He didn't want her?

Chase put his hands back to his temples and closed his eyes. "I don't want to think about you every day. I don't want to wonder what you're thinking about every second of the day. I don't want to wonder what your opinion is on a particular topic and wonder if we'll disagree and how you'll try to change my mind."

He let go of his temple and paced the grass. He marched in a perfect line, back erect, head up high. The perfect soldier.

"I don't want to think about kissing you every second. I don't want to actually kiss you because then I'll know. I'll know, and I'll want to do it again and again."

He stopped marching and about-faced, which brought him right to her. He glared down at her, brown eyes accusing. But his voice softened.

"I don't want to want you because you're the kind of girl that a man doesn't stop wanting once he's caught her."

Ginger ran her hands through her hair. She pressed at the throb in her temple. "I'm so confused."

Chase let out a soft chuckle. "Well, I'll bet that's a first."

He grinned down at her. Which only served to make her even more confused. Was he telling her he wanted her? Or that he didn't? There were so many double negatives in his statement she had no idea where she stood. She was completely lost.

Chase looked lost too. He raised his hand and rubbed at his forehead. Ginger reached for him, placing her fingers over his.

"Is it back?" she asked. "Are you feeling okay?"

Chase let his hand drop but not to his side. His palm cupped her face. The moment his skin touched hers, that delicious warmth that seemed to come from somewhere deep in him spread all through her.

"No," he said. "I'm not okay. I am so far gone."

His lips brushed hers. Lightly at first. Just a taste. Then, just as he predicted, he took another and then another kiss.

And so it went until the crickets began to chirp, and the other night creatures crawled out of their hovels and announced their presence. Ginger and Chase ignored them all as they clung to one another. When they finally broke apart, they both were very clear on where they stood.

But they decided not to let any of the other residents of the ranch know that the two of them were now a sure bet.

CHAPTER FIFTEEN

"*L*adies and gentlemen, please welcome your next state senator, Ginger Dumasse."

The crowd's applause thundered in Chase's ears. He ignored it in favor of the sweetness on his lips. The voters gathered in the union hall whooped and hollered for Ginger. They could yell, shout, and clap for her to come on stage all they wanted. Backstage, Chase had her in his arms and was not letting her go any time soon.

His palm cradled the nape of Ginger's neck. He used his thumb to tilt her chin up for better access to her perfect lips. He tried to only sip, to pace himself.

That plan failed. Chase took healthy gulps of her. He couldn't get enough. He knew he'd never be able to get enough of the spicy-sweet taste of this woman.

"I know she's back there," said Carla from the

stage. There was a tinge of annoyance in her voice. "Maybe a bit more applause will get her out here. Let's show Councilwoman Dumasse that we believe she will be our next senator. Put your hands together, people!"

Chase latched his hands onto Ginger. He laced their fingers as he continued to take from her lips. But the louder applause got to Ginger. She squirmed in Chase's hold as duty called her.

With great effort, Chase tore his lips from hers. His mouth obeyed, but his hands refused to cooperate. One by one, he peeled his fingers off her. But as his pinky left her, he dipped down for another kiss.

"You two, get a room," Carla hissed from the curtain separating the stage from the back of the platform.

Chase finally let Ginger go. He did it with a cheeky grin that said he would do it again if he got a chance. Ginger showed no remorse either.

"Or," Carla grinned, her gaze going shrewd, "he could put a ring on it. Everyone loves an engagement."

"We're not getting married," said Ginger. "We've only just started dating."

She said the words adamantly, even crossing her arms over her chest. Something about the phrase didn't sit well with Chase. The statement simply didn't sound true.

Ginger looked up at him. There was a hint of doubt in her clear blue eyes. "We *are* dating, aren't we?"

In response, Chase leaned down and stole one more kiss. "Dinner tonight?"

She nodded. The doubt was gone from her gaze, replaced with a dreamy look.

"Come on." Carla yanked her away. "You've got a job to do."

Ginger went with her campaign manager, but grudgingly. Her gaze was still on Chase. "Wait for me?"

Chase couldn't form words. Well, he could. He just wasn't ready for her to hear them. Or perhaps he wasn't ready to admit them to himself.

At that moment, Chase knew he'd wait forever for this woman. He realized he had been waiting a lifetime for her. He knew for certain that he would spend a lifetime with her.

He didn't say any of that. He simply nodded at her. Her smile broke open his heart.

Chase was so totally marrying Ginger Dumasse.

Most of her speech brushed over him. He leaned against the wall backstage and took her in. He took in her passion, her conviction, her drive.

A few words of her platform penetrated his mind. His first instinct was to argue with her health care plan. To rebut her proposal on tax reform. To reject her course of action on interstate trade deals.

In the end, he realized the strategies didn't matter. What did was that she wanted the best for the people of this state, and she was prepared to work hard to make their lives better.

Wow, he was completely head over heels for that woman.

Ten minutes after her speech was over, hands were shaken, and pictures taken, she was back in his arms where she belonged. They had pulled up outside her campaign headquarters. The sun lit her face. A small smile played at her lips. Chase could've stared at her all day.

"You did really well back there," he said.

She preened at his compliment, snuggling into his hold as she leaned into him from the passenger seat. "They believed me."

"Because you told the truth. You're a novelty; a politician that speaks truth to power."

She turned her head into his chest, so he couldn't see her features, but he felt her mouth spread into a grin. "I just hope it's enough to win."

"You're gonna win."

"How do you know that?" She tilted her head back and gazed up at him.

Chase ran his index finger down the side of her face. "Politics isn't about the issues. It's about the people. Even when you disagree with people, you've proven that you'll listen. That's really what they want; someone who listens to them."

"Are you speaking for yourself, Sergeant?"

"I think I know the will of the people."

Ginger tugged her lower lip in her mouth. Chase had to grit his teeth. If he started kissing her now, he wouldn't stop. They were parked on the street. Even now, someone might be snapping a picture for tomorrow's headlines.

"You should go to work before I'm charged with abducting a government employee," he said. "That would not look good on my rap sheet."

Ginger brought his hand to her lips and kissed his knuckles. "Thank you."

"What for?"

"For supporting me, even when you don't agree with me."

"We have a lot more in common than we differ."

"I'm coming to see that."

Ginger smiled again. Something squeezed in Chase's chest, likely the very last objection to spending forever with this woman. She was going to be late for her next appointment. They both were. Chase threw caution to the wind and captured her lips.

Just as he was about to deepen the kiss and make them both even more late, a knock sounded at the passenger side window.

"You two should know you have an audience," said Carla.

Chase looked over to see photographers

snapping away. He shrugged and gave Ginger one more kiss before letting her get out of the car. They were together, and he wanted everyone to know it.

He watched her walk up the steps, making sure she got inside the building before starting his engine. Though his engines were already raring to go. His head was clear, and his heart was full, and he could not remember how he'd gone from happily single to enthusiastically in a committed relationship in what? Two days? That had to be a Purple Heart Ranch record. He doubted anyone of the soldiers or wives had bet on those odds.

Pulling into the recruitment center, Chase saw a luxury car parked out front. Standing at the front of the car was a large man smoking an expensive cigar. Ice cold washed over the warm feeling in his body. Chase knew the man.

"Mr. Dumasse," Chase said as he came out of the car.

The man didn't bother with a preamble. "We need to talk about you dating my daughter."

He hadn't expected this. From what he'd seen with Henry Dumasse's treatment of his youngest daughter, Honey, and what Ginger had told him about her father, Chase doubted the man would care what his eldest daughter got up to.

But it looked like he was wrong. Maybe Dumasse had a change of heart. Still, what was happening between Chase and Ginger was not the man's business.

"Ginger is a grown woman," said Chase. "She can determine who she dates."

"This has nothing to do with dating," said Dumasse. "It's about the campaign, and what my endorsement will do for Ginger. That is if you play ball."

CHAPTER SIXTEEN

"Ginger, David Jacobs from Charbury Academy is calling, should I take a message?"

"Yeah," said Ginger automatically.

She'd been operating on autopilot since Chase handed her out of his car. She'd never felt more alive than when she was in his arms, and he was holding her, kissing her. Agreeing with her that she would make an amazing leader because she listened.

"You know what?" Ginger said as her assistant was nearly out of the door. "I should invite Mr. Jacobs to lunch."

Her assistant blinked. She gave her head a waggle, like a dog who was uncertain of its human's command. "All right … I guess I'll find time in your schedule?"

"You do that," said Ginger. "He and I should meet face to face and work our issues out."

Ginger's door was wide open. The campaign office was usually filled with chatter. People working the phones and talking to constituents to get votes. People typing away on keyboards, posting to social media. People chatting with each other, discussing the latest issue and how to solve the problems of the world.

If it hadn't been for the abrupt and total silence, Ginger may not have ever noticed something was the matter.

Phones dangled from earlobes like loosened earrings. Fingers were held suspended in the air over keyboards. Mouths gaped open, hanging mutely in mid-sentence. All gazes were wide as they focused on her.

"What did I say?" Ginger asked no one in particular.

Carla ushered her assistant out and came into the office. She closed the door and turned to face Ginger. "What has gotten into you, girl? Or rather, should I say who?"

"Don't be crass, Carla." Ginger rounded her desk and plopped into her seat. She didn't face Carla. She swiveled her chair until it faced the window. The clouds were particularly fluffy today, with swirls and swoops like a pillow. She'd bet they'd be just as soft, like a lover's kiss. "We've only just started dating."

She was dating Chase. He'd said as much. What was she going to wear tonight for dinner? Maybe she should go and buy a new outfit? First, she needed to clean her apartment. It was a mess. Not that he'd be staying over or anything. They were only dating.

"Gin, I'm happy that you finally have someone in your life because goodness knows, you needed a man."

"Hey." Ginger swiveled back around to face her friend.

"The soldier has my approval. But," Carla held up a finger, "not if he's going to change everything you stand for."

"He hasn't. He can't. Chase isn't like that."

"You just agreed to a sit down with the assistant principal of a private school who is diametrically opposed to your platform on public education."

"Because that's the adult thing to do. The two of us have an issue. We should sit down face to face and talk it out like mature, grown people."

Carla reared back as if Ginger's words were throwing daggers. "In what world would that work?"

"In the real world," Ginger insisted. "Not this hyper-polarized world we all are imagining is the real thing. Nothing is working with everyone in their own corners. We need to come to the middle and actually meet."

"Huh." Carla pursed her lips. Then she took out her phone and began tapping away.

"Who are you texting?" asked Ginger.

"I'm not texting. I'm writing all that down. It's going to go great in your next speech."

Ginger sighed, but then she rose and rounded the desk. She sat on the edge and hugged her friend.

"Really?" asked Carla. "Is the soldier's loving that good?"

"Yeah," Ginger grinned.

Not that Chase had made any declarations of love to her. It was way too soon for that. Too soon for her to even feel anything close to love. Definitely too early to be planning the cut of her wedding dress, or where they might live, or what their children's names would be.

Just tell all that to her overactive heart. The thing pounded just at the mention of his name. Yes, she did have it bad …and it was so good.

Chase had shown her another side of himself last night on the ranch. He'd shown his vulnerable side. It had been painful to watch him suffer, but that episode had broken down the remaining walls between them. It was clear he trusted her enough to let her hold him during his time of need.

"I don't have to change who I am just because I'm with someone who is on a different side of an issue than me. I think just being with Chase has made me stronger. You know the saying; iron sharpens iron. Right?"

"I have no idea," said Carla. "I use a service to

sharpen my kitchen knives. I have no idea how they do it."

"Trust me, that's how they do it," said Ginger. "If all we ever do is try to get strong in a group of like-minded people, we won't get any stronger. It all would get dull soon."

"So, you're changing your platform?"

"I'm not changing the platform." Ginger took a deep breath as she realized the truth. "I've changed. I'm open to listening to others and making the platform stronger by running it up against ideas that aren't wholly mine. We'd leave a whole section of the community out if I got one-hundred percent of what I wanted. There's enough room for some give. With the give as well as the take, everyone gets some of what they want. It'll make the platform stronger if more people are included."

Carla took a deep breath herself. Ginger waited, her own breath baited. Luckily, her friend and campaign manager bit.

"Okay," said Carla. "I'm with you."

Once again, the two friends hugged it out.

"What's going on up at that ranch?" said Carla. "Maybe I need to pay them a visit, get a soldier of my own."

Before Ginger could respond, a knock sounded at the door. Her assistant poked her head in.

"Ginger, there's a Mr. Chase to see you."

And there her heart went again. They hadn't

been apart for ten minutes, and he was already coming back for more. But when her assistant moved aside, it was a gray-haired man that darkened the doorway. He had Chase's face but under a number of wrinkles. And the smile was wrong. It was predatory.

"Ms. Dumasse, I'm Lloyd Chase. I believe you are acquainted with my son."

CHAPTER SEVENTEEN

"It's simple, son," said Henry Dumasse, the man also known as the Sugar Daddy due to his family's sugar plantation.

Dumasse moved his large frame around Chase's office, neither sitting or standing still. He sprinkled his presence all over the room, touching surfaces and glaring at the furniture. He was the sugary sprinkles on top of a healthy fruit salad, completely out of place.

None of that chafed as much as the last word Dumasse had uttered. Chase did not like being called son. Not by this man. Not even by his own father. It had even rankled when drill sergeants had said the word.

Chase never used it when he was doling out orders to his own soldiers. He gave them more respect than that. If you survived boot camp, you were a full-fledged man or woman. Not a child.

"My daughter is not going to win this race," said Dumasse.

Chase grit his teeth. Wasn't there a rule that parents had to support their kids? Not just financially but spiritually, socially, in their dreams. The other men in his squad had come from excellent homes where their parents cheered them on.

But not Dylan Banks. Dylan's parents, who were New York socialites, hadn't spoken to him since he lost his leg in combat. Maybe it was rich people's problems?

"Norman Dean has too many endorsements for her to have any real impact," her father was saying.

Maybe that was it? Maybe money was the corrupting factor? Chase and Ginger came from wealth, but they were both good people. They'd also both walked away from that wealth and struck out on their own.

"Meanwhile, my daughter has cornered the youth and mommy blogger vote."

It was a shame. Chase's own parents hadn't believed in him. They hadn't been in support of the way he wanted to live his life in service to his country rather than to the family business. They couldn't see that service to his country was serving his family.

"Dean is too well connected in this community," Dumasse continued his disparaging tirade against his daughter's chances at success in the race.

Chase begged to differ with that last statement. He hadn't seen Norman Dean out in the community, other than his face on a glossy poster at a bus stop. Chase had seen pictures of Dean at fancy dinners in newspapers and in negative television ads.

The man had never gotten his hands dirty in the trenches like Ginger. Dean hadn't visited the schools and seen the plight of teachers. He hadn't been on ranches and farms and seen the conditions of the laborers. He hadn't been to factories and seen the conditions of those workers.

But Ginger had. Not only that, but she had a plan to help each person in this community find their next level of success. True, Chase didn't believe in every one of those plans. But he'd stand behind her and hold her up while she tried to make her vision work. Because he believed in *her*.

"She needs a high-level endorsement if she has any hope of beating him," said Dumasse.

"Well, seeing as she already has her father's endorsement, I'm not sure how much higher she could get."

Chase was surprised he got the statement out with a straight face. He held his features still while he waited for Dumasse's reaction. Ginger's father glared at him.

Chase glared right back. He had no idea what was about to come out of the man's mouth, but he knew he wouldn't like it. He also knew he wouldn't stand here and listen to much more of this vitriol about the woman he believed in, the woman who was the right choice to lead this community, the woman he loved.

"My daughter and I have never seen eye to eye," said Dumasse. "We are on the opposite sides of most issues. I have every reason to believe the two of you are opposites in most respects, as well."

Again, Chase held his tongue still and kept his face blank. He would give nothing away to this man. But in the end, he had to know. "What do you want, Mr. Dumasse?"

"Let me make myself plain, son. I'll support my daughter's candidacy if you broker a deal with your father."

Chase's blank expression turned fierce. Was that what this was about? A business deal? Dumasse was going to sell his daughter out over money. Too bad he had the wrong Chase.

"I have no say in my father's business," said Chase.

"You're his son."

"She's your daughter," Chase countered. "See how that works."

Dumasse took a deep inhale. He was clearly

trying for patience. Chase bet the man wasn't used to hearing the word no.

"Your father has always thought he was too good to do business with me. Industry folk have always thought themselves too good to get their hands dirty with agriculture. But my money is just as old as his."

Chase didn't bother to engage in this age-old debate. Money was money. It wasn't good or bad. It wasn't even old or new. It was just an indication of how much an individual or group hoarded their part of the pie. Chase had learned in the Army that it wasn't every man for himself. If he didn't have his brothers' back, they'd all fall.

"She's down in the polls," said Dumasse.

"Not anymore. She's rising."

"For how long? There's one point I agree with my daughter on; at the end of the day, this community is about family. What does it look like that her own father won't endorse her?"

Chase had some choice words of what that looked like.

"Think of it like this," Dumasse continued, completely oblivious to Chase's rising ire, "you'll be bringing two families back together."

That was just it. Chase wanted nothing to do with his father. He wanted nothing to do with Ginger's father, either.

But he did want her to win.

"It's just a phone call," said Dumasse.

But that was it. It wasn't just a phone call. Anyone dealing with his father would get up with the short end of the stick. It was the way the man worked.

CHAPTER EIGHTEEN

"You're pretty, at least."

The man before her looked her up and down like she was a car he was considering purchasing. Ginger fought the urge to cross her arms over her chest. Had Ginger heard Mr. Chase right? Her head must still be full from thinking about Chase's kisses. That couldn't have been what Chase's dad just said to her.

"I beg your pardon?" she said, hoping in vain for some clarification.

"Good figure." Mr. Chase tilted his head and regarded her from a different angle. "Nice enough face. You'll do."

Ginger Dumasse was rarely at a loss for words. But as she ran his over and over again in her head, she couldn't get past them. He wasn't hitting on her, thank goodness. He was evaluating her, assessing her quality like some piece of meat. It was so much worse.

"If my family is going to shift political parties for the woman my son is going to be with," Mr. Chase continued, "she at least better be pretty. Politics are changeable. Ugly grandbabies are not an option."

Bile rose in her mouth. Ice shivered down to the base of her spine. Her fingertips went numb.

Ginger wanted to protest that she wouldn't be having Lloyd Chase's grandbabies. More important, that if she did, they would be the most beautiful babies on the planet because they would be a part of Chase and not this ugly man that stood in front of her.

The truth was, Ginger knew she was going to have Lloyd Chase's grandbabies. She'd already had the daydreams. She'd already picked out the names. She'd already planned the ceremony for the day that she would become Mrs. Colin Chase.

No, scratch that. Mrs. Ginger Dumasse-Chase.

But all she said to the despicable man darkening her doorway was, "Chase isn't here. And knowing that he has no relationship with you, I have no intention of telling you where he is."

Chase hadn't spoken much about his parents. Just enough to let her know that they shared the same disdain for the men who had donated half the spark that brought about their existence. Meeting

Lloyd Chase in person, Ginger wondered if she was being too harsh on her own father.

"Oh, I know where my boy is," said Mr. Chase. "He's either on that charity ranch for cripples or at the ridiculous center of his to recruit more lambs to the slaughter. It's you, I'm here to see."

"I have nothing to say to you."

Ginger was so disgusted by this man that she stepped around him and reached for the door. She didn't want to spend any more time in his presence than necessary. She might be the new girlfriend, but making a good impression on such a bad man was not in the cards. Besides, she doubted Chase would disapprove.

"Good," said Mr. Chase, ignoring the open door. "I'm not interested in what you have to say. Only what you can do for me."

"I'm not doing anything for you. Do you really believe I would after you come into my office and insult me?"

Mr. Chase looked bored. "Are you quite done? I have to be back on my private jet in an hour to make a business meeting."

She was not. She balled her hand into a fist and wished she was a man. If she were, she could sock him in his arrogant nose.

Wait? Did her gender matter here? She did stand on a platform of gender equality. So, maybe she could sock him in the nose ...

"I can't stand a woman who has too many opinions," said Mr. Chase. "But, having you come into the family will soften that image of me, which is good for business. Too bad your family line is one of field workers."

This guy couldn't be for real. He was the live caricature of every misogynist screen or book villain come to life. How had Chase come from this?

"You're not going to win this race," said Mr. Chase.

The absolute audacity.

Ginger slammed her door shut. She didn't want any of her staff to witness the act of violence she was about to perform. Before she could ball her hand into a fist, Mr. Chase continued.

"Norman Dean is up in the polls. He has more money, more endorsements, more testosterone."

Ginger truly doubted that last one but whatever. "In case you haven't noticed, my poll numbers are up and rising."

"Not fast enough. It's simple math, sweetie."

Yup, she was socking him in the nose. The assault charges would be worth it. The women's liberation movement simply demanded this act of civil disobedience.

"I'll endorse your campaign," said Mr. Chase.

"Thank you. But, no thank you. Your vote doesn't count, seeing as you don't even live in this state."

"No, but I have tons of workers who do live here.

They could make a dent in your campaign numbers. I own the C&C Factory."

The C&C Factory? The one that was in danger of moving out of state. Lloyd Chase was the out of state shell company. It all made sense now.

Be that as it may, there was still a more important matter on her agenda. "I don't buy votes."

"No, but I'm sure you want your constituents to all still have a job after your election. I can close that plant if I don't get my way."

Now, the ice down her back turned to a blazing fire. "You wouldn't."

"Try me." Lloyd Chase crossed his arms over his chest. He looked absolutely nothing like his son. Both his brows were lowered. His lips were pursed, not in a stern manner. In a devil may care manner.

Ginger was sure this devil didn't care about anyone but himself.

"All I want is for you to work your feminine wiles to get my son to come back to the company."

"You want Chase to come and work for you?"

"You're not the brightest bulb, are you? Yes, that's what I said. This military career looked good when he was young. But now, my shareholders are starting to question the viability of my business. All sons come back to work for their father's company. If Chase doesn't, people will think something is wrong, and my stocks will drop."

This was ludicrous. He wanted her to convince

Chase to give up something he loved and come work for a man he didn't even like. Even if she wanted to, they'd only just started dating today. She didn't have that kind of sway with him. She couldn't even get him to change his mind on sports.

"The clock is ticking, Ms. Dumasse. If my son isn't on the company payroll by the election, then I see no reason to keep C&C Factory in Montana."

hase peered down at the limp noodles on his plate. He separated the vegetables, lining up the broccoli on one side and the carrots on the other. It would be a weak assault for either side. The diced carrots began at a disadvantage being chopped in circular discs and halved into tiny triangles. The broccoli florets were drooping in the marinara.

"How's the pasta?"

Chase lifted his gaze, and all the fight went out of him. When he saw the beautiful woman seated across from him, he put down his knife and fork. All the days' stresses and strains washed away with just a single glance of Ginger.

"The pasta is perfectly cooked," he said. Not that he had first-hand experience. He hadn't taken a single bite. "How's the steak?"

The thick slab of meat sat untouched on her plate. Like his, her hands were bare of utensils. Her arms were crossed over her chest, her fingers worried the sleeve of her shirt.

"It smells delicious," she said.

Ginger picked up her knife and fork. She sliced a piece. The meat gave easily, and the brown char gave way to a pink interior. She popped the bloody morsel into her mouth. Chase couldn't tear his gaze from her lips as she chewed. He would trade places with that cow in a heartbeat.

"Perfectly medium-rare," she said.

"Really? It still looks like it's mooing to me."

"That's how I like my meat. You want a salad with that pasta, lightweight?"

Chase chuckled. He loved how she always flipped the script on him. Here he was eating a dainty pasta dish while she threw down with meat and potatoes. Life would never be dull with Ginger Dumasse. And Chase planned to spend as much of his life with her as possible.

He just had to figure out how to do it with her slime bag of a father out of the picture.

There was no way Chase was selling Ginger out. He may not be in line behind all of her positions. But his main position was firm; he would always stand behind Ginger. He'd stand beside her when she needed support. He'd stand in front of her when she needed protection.

He vowed here and now that he would always be there for her regardless of where they stood on an issue. Because even when she had it wrong, her heart always was in the right place. He could not say the same for Henry Dumasse.

Chase rubbed at his head. The nagging of a headache was at the crown of his temple. Before it could creep around his skull, something cool and soothing touched his forehead.

Ginger.

With the pads of her fingers, she began a wiping motion. Her gentle care was too much artillery for the migraine. With each brush, with each press, with each caress, the dull ache receded.

Chase wanted to rest his whole head in her hands. Not just his head, his heart, his very soul. But he couldn't. They were out in public.

From his peripheral vision, he saw people staring at them. There were no flashes of bulbs. No whispers from behind cupped hands. No, instead, the other diners smiled at them. Clearly, they had this crowd's approval.

Chase lifted his head. He took Ginger's fingers in his hand. One by one, he kissed each one of her fingertips, then her knuckles.

"Is your headache back?" she asked.

"They're migraines," he admitted. "I get them from time to time."

"I hear they come when someone is stressed."

Chase turned Ginger's hands over and pressed his lips into first her right palm and then her left. "It was stressful in combat zones."

"You're not in a combat zone any longer," she said.

"I'm not?" He looked up at her with a grin.

Ginger returned his grin. She still held his face in her hands. Her thumbs brushed his lips. Not in a way that he felt silenced. In a way, he felt acknowledged, understood, accepted.

Her gaze was so full of compassion and care that Chase felt undone, unmanned. All of his defenses came crashing down at the words of this woman. Had they been adversaries only a couple of days ago?

"Is there something else going on?" she asked. "Something stressing you out."

Chase wrapped his fingers around hers, taking over the caretaker role. He was the one who was supposed to protect her. And that's exactly what he intended to do.

"I just had a trying day," he said.

"Do you want to talk about it?"

No. He would not concern her with what a degenerate her father was. He'd figure out a way to fix this.

If he was honest with himself, he had an idea of how to fix it. That's what was bringing on the migraine. The stress he was about to endure with his plan.

"I'd rather talk about your day," he said. "Anything interesting happened after I left the campaign offices?"

"No." Ginger slid her fingers from his hands. She picked up her knife and fork and sawed into her steak. "Nothing interesting. Just the same old politics."

Something crossed her features. Her blue eyes churned, like the sea in a storm. But her smile was cool, calm, like the eye of a hurricane. He could see the wheels turning in her mind. He just had no idea where they were blowing.

Her gaze met his again. There was something that looked like need in her eyes. Impulsively, he reached for her again, needing her to know that he was there for her.

She let him take her hand. He pressed their palms together, needing to feel the center of her. She squeezed back.

"We're on the same side now," she said. "Well, not with political, social, or economic issues."

"No," Chase chuckled. "Not with any of those. But I always have your back. I want you to know that."

"And I've got yours."

CHAPTER TWENTY

"You sure you want to do this, Gin?"

Ginger sat back in the passenger seat of Honey's truck. Her little sister used to drive a luxury car. No, scratch that. Her little sister used to be driven around town in luxury cars. Now, she was behind the wheel of a rusty pickup truck.

The air conditioner didn't work, so they'd rolled the windows down. Honey's normally coiffed hair was pulled back in a ponytail. Loose strands flew around her bare face. She wasn't wearing a stitch of makeup, except maybe Chapstick. And she was dressed in worn jeans, with mud on the knees, and dingy work boots.

Out of designer heels and tailored cocktail dresses, Honey was thriving. She'd married a man who showed her the love she deserved. She was surrounded by a tribe of people who nurtured and looked out for her. And yet, they were parked outside of the loneliest, most soul-crushing place on earth.

The Dumasse estate.

"Yes," said Ginger. "I have to do this."

However, Ginger's hand hesitated on the door handle. Instead, she reached over and swallowed her sister in a hug. They both had survived this place and come out the other end awesome individuals. It proved that where you came from didn't have to determine the rest of your life. People failed and succeeded based on their will and perseverance, not their circumstances.

Honey reached for the door handle when Ginger released her.

"No," said Ginger. "You stay here. If I'm not out in twenty minutes, then you can charge through the door."

"You don't have to tell me twice." Honey twisted her watch to face her. She clicked a few dials. "Clock's ticking."

Ginger giggled at the fierce look in her sister's gaze, a gaze so much like their mother's. The two had been estranged for most of Honey's life when Honey chose to stay with their father in the divorce instead of coming to live with Ginger and their mom in a downsized apartment on the fringe of the middle class. But neither Ginger or their mom had ever stopped reaching out for Honey. She only wished their mom was here to see Honey blossom into the strong, confident, and capable woman she'd become.

Ginger climbed out of the truck and made her way up the steps to her ancestral home. The doors to the manse opened for her automatically. She had wondered if she would be welcomed back after her last run-in with her father when she told him she never wanted to see him again.

She'd meant it at the time. He'd tried to sell Honey's hand in marriage off to profit his business. It was despicable.

Luckily, it was the worst thing he could do. He couldn't slip any lower. The plan she'd formulated to counter Lloyd Chase's request would be the last chance her own father had at redemption. If he didn't rise to this occasion, she would not be coming back again.

Ginger walked the halls of the house to his office. She knew that's where he'd be. That's where he always was. When she had a school performance. When they were having family dinner. When she had a nightmare. This was where he always was.

Like every time before when she'd needed him, and he wasn't there, she found him here. Henry Dumasse sat behind his desk. There was a mountain of papers piled high. Unlike his contemporaries, the Sugar Daddy preferred paper to digital.

"Dad?"

He looked up, confusion on his brow. Perhaps at the title, she'd called him? Or at the interruption in general? She would never be sure. It wasn't what she was here to ask him.

"Hi," she said.

Her father frowned. He didn't put down the stack of papers in his hand. Of course, he didn't. Like when she was a girl, her interruptions, her seeking of his affections, was not welcome. She might as well get to the point.

Ginger took a few steps into the room. She didn't invite herself to sit down. She stood before him and presented her platform like she would any other person whose vote she wanted.

"I have a proposition for you," she said.

Wonder upon wonder, he sat his papers down. But not his pen. That, he kept in his hand, clicking the balled point out, then in. Ginger decided to take the small victory. Her father leaned back and regarded her with something that looked like interest.

"You know the company C&C Factory?" It wasn't really a question. She knew he knew of it. He knew of every business in this town that wasn't his. "I happen to know that it's going to be up for sale soon. I have it on good authority that the shareholders are going to get antsy over some poor dynamics between the owner and his son."

Lloyd Chase was certainly not going to like the dynamic of Ginger ignoring his request to get Chase to work for him. Chase's happiness was far too important to her to put him in a miserable situation as working for that man. But she still needed to save the jobs of the people in this community. She just hoped this plan would work. It should. It appealed to her father's greed.

"I've run the numbers," she continued, "and the profit margin is good. I think you should consider buying it and taking it over."

"So, he came and talked to you, did he?"

Her father's grin was predatory. It was the look she'd seen him give the rare times he'd discussed business at the dinner table. He was most happy when he was preparing to take a business down. It was the same look on his face during the divorce trial.

Ginger got a bad feeling in her stomach. Her father knew Lloyd Chase had come to her? Did he know about the estrangement between Chase and his father? If her father did know, he'd likely side with the elder Chase. Henry Dumasse had never forgiven Ginger for what he considered abandoning the family. All the more reason to keep Chase out of business with these two men and pit them against one another.

"So, you and Mr. Chase discussed this already?" asked Ginger.

"*Mister* Chase? Not the father, the son. Chase, the boy. The soldier."

Wait? What? "Sergeant Chase? You spoke to Chase?"

What had her father been doing speaking to Chase? More importantly, why hadn't Chase come to her and tell her about it?

"I told the boy I wanted him to put me in touch with his father. That pompous man hasn't returned any of my calls. I've been trying to work a deal with him for months now. But you say there's a weak spot in one of his businesses?"

Her father picked up a blank sheet of paper. He began scribbling on it in his unintelligible chicken scratch. But Ginger didn't need to read his words to know that he was planning a takeover.

What had she done? Her mind went back to the people at her rally, those who worked in the factory. They were about to be at the mercy of one or the other of these men who didn't care enough about their own families. They certainly weren't going to give a care to people they didn't know.

This had been a mistake. In her bid to protect Chase, she'd only traded one devil for the other. But why hadn't Chase told her about her father's talk with him?

Probably for the same reason she hadn't told Chase about his father coming to her. They were trying to protect each other.

The door to her father's office burst open, and a blonde tornado darkened the doorway.

"It's been twenty minutes," Honey said as she glared at their father. "I'm here to rescue you."

Of course, she was. Because that's what real family and friends did. That's what community did. Regardless of where they stood, they all protected one another. Ginger quickly formulated a new plan to do the same.

CHAPTER TWENTY-ONE

Montana mountains gave way to Spokane rain. It had been a long time since Chase had been back home to Washington state. The long drive helped to clear his head and get his mind straight. Still, the blue clouds in the sky reminded him of a certain blonde's gaze when she was on a stage and owning a crowd.

Ginger was never far from Chase's mind these days. Last night, after dinner, he'd left her at her door. It wasn't the marinara that had been on his tongue as he'd gone to sleep. It had been that sweet-spicy taste of her.

She'd invaded his dreams and was working her way into each chamber of his heart. He was determined to protect her from her villain of a father. Hence, the need to leave the state.

Chase pushed his foot down on the gas pedal.

He could've flown and made the trip home faster. But he needed the time and space away from Ginger. His instincts to protect her were growing stronger each day. He hated that he wasn't telling her the whole truth, aka lying to her. She had enough on her plate. This was a burden he could handle.

Five hours later, on a road trip that should've taken nearly eight hours, he parked in the driveway of his parents' house. He let loose the seatbelt and waited for the migraine to take him.

But his head was steady. He was doing the right thing. And when he was done righting this wrong, he got to go back and be with the woman he was falling in love with.

Ginger had a campaign rally later tonight. Chase was determined to be there for her. To show everyone that she had his support, even if they didn't see eye to eye. She was the best man for the job.

"You want me to come in with you?" Ortega asked from the passenger seat.

"No," said Chase. "You don't need to witness this. But if I'm not out in twenty minutes, call for reinforcements."

He gave his friend a complicated handshake and then climbed out of the car. It had been years since he'd climbed the steps to his parents' front door. The military had provided an excellent excuse to stay away. Now that his service was over, and he lived just one state away, he had no excuse not to come home every once in a while.

The door opened, and his mother stood on the other side. "Colin, darling. What are you doing with your hair?"

Chase ran a hand over his short-cropped cut. It was habit. His mother was all about keeping up appearances.

"I thought you'd let it grow back now that you're out of the Navy."

"Army, Mother. And I still work for the military. I'm a recruiter."

"Are you sure, darling?" Annabelle Chase's brows pinched in distaste as she looked everywhere but in her son's eyes. "Your father told me you were coming back to the family business."

Back? Chase had never been in the family business. But his mother rarely concerned herself with the facts of his life.

"I hear you're dating? The girl is from a wealthy family? But it's farming, I hear?"

Chase balled his hands into fists so that he wouldn't pinch the bridge of his nose. He was surprised he hadn't inherited his mother's snobbishness. It was likely because she'd never held him as a baby. She'd left that to nannies.

"But I don't know about her character. She takes on things outside her gender. How will I know she can take care of you the way you need, darling?"

Seemed they were getting the gossip rags from Montana here in Washington.

"Mother, Ginger is an amazing woman. She makes me a stronger man. She challenges me, and pushes me hard to do better, be better. She makes me the best version of myself. How could you want more for your son?"

His mother frowned at him as though he'd just spoken another language. Chase knew it was a waste of time. His mother had only ever aspired to be a trophy on a rich man's arm. Chase had always aspired to be in the heart of a woman with an indomitable spirit. Both their wishes had come true. Though Chase appeared to be the only one of them happy about the turn of events.

"Colin, there you are, my boy."

The vein in Chase's temple popped. But still, there was no aching pain starting in his skull. He turned to face his father.

Lloyd Chase was not aging well. His cheeks looked hallow but bright. Not a healthy bright. More like a plastic kind of bright. He wondered if his father had traveled south to the surgeons of California?

"It's about time you got here. Your first order of business will be to help me unravel this mess."

"What mess is that?"

"The mess with the Dumasses."

His father slumped into a chair. Chase remained

standing. This conversation wasn't starting the way he'd planned.

His father thought he was coming to work for him? There was a conflict with the Dumasses? And not one, but two of them? He knew his father wasn't talking about Honey. Mark's wife was happily up to her knees in dirt back on the ranch.

"When I went and spoke to that girl of yours, I thought I made myself clear," his father was saying.

"You went to see Ginger?" Chase felt a prickle at the back of his knees. The prickle urged him to sit down for what was to come. He didn't dare get too close to his father. He wasn't entirely sure patricide wasn't on the table.

"Of course, I did," said the old man. "How else would she know about the C&C Factory?"

The C&C Factory? Chase didn't keep abreast of his family's holdings. The Chase family holdings were a massive empire that spanned many states. It was likely that his father owned the factory back in Montana. The picture was still a blur, but the edges were slowly sharpening.

"Now her ape, who thinks he's a sugar baron, is trying to buy me out."

"You're selling a factory in Montana?"

"No," his father huffed, eying Chase like he was an idiot. A look Chase had become used to in his childhood. "I was never going to sell. Downsize, sure. But the deal I made with that girl of yours was just to get your attention, to get you back into the fold."

Everything was becoming clear. Still, Chase's vision blurred nonetheless. His father had tried to use Ginger to get him to come into the business.

Chase wasn't angry.

He was numb.

Here, he'd come to warn his father that Henry Dumasse might have something up his sleeve. Chase had still harbored some loyalty to his family to try and protect them. Meanwhile, his father was trying to blackmail the woman he loved.

But with what?

The moment the question formed in his mind, Chase knew the sickening answer. C&C Factory. The workers had come to Ginger at a rally earlier in the week, asking what she as a candidate could do to protect their jobs. And his father had used that as blackmail.

That's what he'd seen in her eyes the other night. She'd been hiding her knowledge of what a lowbred his father was. Just as he'd been hiding the same knowledge of her father from her.

The two men deserved each other. But the workers didn't deserve either of them. People weren't pawns.

Chase didn't waste his breath on his father. The man wouldn't understand. He was already back-stepping out of the room. He needed to put as much distance between himself and this excuse of a man as possible.

"Wait? Where are you going? If the board doesn't see that you've finally taken your place in the company, they'll think there's something wrong."

"Oh, there's something wrong, all right."

And now, Chase was formulating a plan to right that wrong. He just hoped he could make his bid for change before Henry Dumasse ruined things.

"If you walk out that door, you'll be abandoning your family."

"Nope," said Chase as he crossed the threshold. "I'm going home to my family."

Ginger looked out in the crowd. It was a full house. But she didn't see the one person she wanted to see. Where was he?

"Ginger," called Carla from the side of the stage. "It's time."

Yes, it was time. Time for her to walk her talk. Time for her to put her money where her mouth was. And every other cliché that meant she had to stand firm in her beliefs.

Ginger had been a strong, independent woman before she was of legal age. But today, she wanted to lean on the shoulder of one particular man. She wanted Chase's blessing on this particular plan. She wanted his acknowledgment on what she was about to do. She wanted his support.

But he wasn't here.

She was certain he'd be on her side. At least she

hoped he would. Her actions would severely tick off his father.

"Gin?"

Unfortunately, Ginger couldn't stall any longer. She stepped onto the makeshift stage inside the C&C Factory. They'd moved their campaign rally here at the last minute. The workers here needed to hear what she had to say as they were about to be impacted by her announcement.

Applause greeted her as she looked out at the crowd. There was a mix of people. Most of the crowd were workers in their blue overalls. There were also moms with babies on their hips or toddlers in hand. A large group of coeds held up snazzy signs. There was even a nice sized group of men and women in business suits leaning against one of the walls. Standing at the front, where she could see them, was a large party from the Purple Heart Ranch.

From the cradle of her husband's embrace, Maggie winked at her. Eva and Reegan both gave her the thumbs up. Honey and Mark whooped and hollered the loudest.

Ginger couldn't help but feel a sense of pride well in her chest. This was the coalition she'd wanted to build. These were the people of the town, her community.

"I've got some good news and bad news," she began. "The bad news is that the plant is changing ownership."

A ripple of surprise went through the crowd like a heatwave. Just as soon as the room heated up, a cold wind of reality breezed over everyone. Ginger could feel despair settling in like dark clouds. She rushed on to show everyone that the sun was on the horizon. Or at least it would be. Once she enacted her plan.

"The good news is that I've decided to purchase the factory with the remaining monies of my inheritance."

Another ripple went through the crowd. This time it was as though night turned to day. Heads that had bowed in expectation of dark times lifted, a new ray of hope dawned in their eyes.

Ginger had spent the morning on the phones with a financial planner and lawyer. They had already started negotiations with C&C Factory's board of directors. There was only one snag. There was another buyer in the mix, but Ginger was prepared to raise her offer. That other buyer didn't know who they were messing with. She wasn't about to let another shell company, which was nothing but an absentee parent, move into her community and wreak havoc. They'd all had enough uncertainty.

"I've been a part of this community all my life," she said. "It's invested in me. From the teachers in the public school system to the pastors in church, to the leaders in the recreational centers. I would not be here today if it wasn't for my neighbors. Win or lose in this election, I plan to be my neighbor's keeper."

A slow golf clap began in the audience. It picked up speed rapidly until the room thundered with applause. But Ginger's eyes had found the epicenter of the beginnings of the growing praise.

Chase.

He stood in the middle of the room. Clapping his capable hands. Smiling that devastating grin. Walking slowly toward her. And then he was there. Standing at the edge of the platform. He stood in front of her, his support of her clear in his warm, brown gaze.

The room had gone silent as the community members looked between the two of them. If people didn't know there was something between her and Chase, they wouldn't be able to mistake it now. The heat coming off them was hotter than a summer day under the Montana sky.

With great difficulty, Ginger tore her gaze away from Chase and faced her constituents. Her job wasn't done. She still had to actually purchase the factory.

"I promise to do everything in my power to win the bid and buy out this company—"

"The factory was sold earlier this afternoon." Chase's deep voice easily carried over her amplified words.

Ginger looked down to Chase. Was she too late? Had their fathers made some under-the-table deal?

Chase climbed onto the stage. He leaned into the mic to speak to the people, but his gaze never left her. "The shell company that owned this factory belonged to my family. Being that I had an interest, and thanks to a bit of nepotism, I was able to take ownership of this factory."

"Chase, you didn't." Ginger placed her hand on his heart. This was the last thing she wanted. She knew Chase didn't want to be in business with his father. All her efforts had been for naught.

"I didn't go into business with my father if that's what you're worried about. I went to the board of directors and purchased the factory directly, using my inheritance."

Ginger reared back. She snatched her hand from his chest. Then she balled her fist and punched him in the shoulder.

"I was going to do that with my inheritance."

Chase chuckled as he caught her fist. He pressed her knuckles to his lips for a sweet kiss. "I'd offer to sell it to you, but seeing as I'm going to make you another offer in the near future—one that would entitle you to fifty percent of everything I own, and one hundred percent of my heart and devotion—I figured it would be a moot point."

For the second time in her life, Ginger was

speechless. She stood on the stage, in the embrace of the strongest, most capable man she knew, and she had no idea, no plan of how to deal with him. For the first time in her life, she was content to simply follow.

"So, we'll be working for both of you?" someone called from the crowd.

"Yes," answered Chase.

"But you two are on opposite sides of most of the issues."

"Not when it comes to family," said Chase. "For both of us, this community, and its people, are family."

"I agree," said Ginger. "It was never about donors, or endorsements, or deals for me. It was always about you. Whether you agree or disagree with me, I'm always going to have your back. I'm always going to fight for you. Because that's what you do for the people you care about, for the people you love."

"I don't know about you," said Chase. "But this woman's certainly got my vote. And my heart."

"Then," she said, "I'm a winner."

Chase brushed his lips against hers. Ginger tilted her head back and accepted his claim. She knew that in the near future, she would accept his ring. She would accept everything about this man. And work her hardest to convert him into a soccer fan.

But that would be for another day.

"Oh, oh, oh! Here's another one."

Ortega had the television remote in his hand. He was clicking through the various local and national news channels for updates on the race. Due to the combined stories of Chase's takeover of the factory his father had owned, and the love story between himself and Ginger, the media outlets had all picked up the story and ran with it.

Good thing too because the story had ticked up Ginger's poll numbers so high that she'd overtaken Norman Dean in the race. They couldn't have planned it better. There were some factions that believed that the two of them had connived their whole affair. Those stories had been put out by the Dean campaign.

But the ring on Ginger's finger, the announcements that had gone out in the mail last week, and their impending nuptials all put a damper on those conspiracy stories. Anyone looking at Chase or Ginger could easily tell that they were madly, deeply, head-over-combat-boots in love.

"She's ahead in the Stokes Poll," said Ortega.

The barn filled with cheers, so loud the rafters shook a bit. The four corners of the room were filled with people from Ginger's campaign, supporters from town, and of course, their family at the Purple Heart Ranch.

Every man, woman, child, and dog had gone to work over the last couple of months for Ginger's campaign. They'd knocked on doors. They'd manned the phones. They'd shouted from the rooftops. And their voices weren't alone.

Ginger's support in the neighboring towns of the district had also risen. So too had Chase's invitations to come and speak at schools and churches and recreational centers about recruitment into the Armed Forces.

It just went to prove that all it took was sincerity, an open mind, and a good heart to get people to listen and have your back.

"Oh, oh, oh," shouted Ortega. "Channel Two is calling it for Dumasse."

The room went insane with applause and whoops. Chase ignored them all as he made his way through the bodies in search of one person in particular.

"Looks like I'm going to win this bet, too," Maggie Banks was saying to Ginger.

Chase had found the two women in the corner of the room. Ginger was surrounded by the brides of Purple Heart Ranch. Even though they hadn't said their *I do's* just yet, she had been inducted into this ever-growing sisterhood. Just as Chase had been drafted into the brotherhood of the males that had started this whole operation.

Surrounding the women in a loose formation were the men of his team. Reece and Brandon sipped from beer bottles as they both gazed at their wives. Dylan and Fran were on the floor, rolling around with the kids and the dogs.

The soldiers and the brides made way for Chase as he marched to Ginger. He swept her in his arms and stole a kiss. As there had been for the last few months of their courtship, there were catcalls and *ahhhs* behind them.

Chase didn't bother turning around to see who was making the ruckus. He knew that his little community here had his back. They were his family as much as the woman in his arms was.

"Nervous?" Chase asked Ginger.

"About what?"

"Looks like you're about to win a state senate seat. That's going to be a lot of responsibility."

Ginger shrugged, her blue eyes bright and filled

with love as she gazed up at him. "I have all the support I need right here."

"And the winner is ..."

Neither of them looked to the television screen as the race was called. Chase pulled Ginger's body into a tighter embrace. As the community cheered around them, Chase and Ginger leaned into each other and shared a kiss that promised commitment and compromise for the rest of their days.

Get ready for more stories from the Purple Heart Ranch.
Be sure and check out
Light Up His Life
the tenth book in The Brides of Purple Heart Ranch
series!

ALSO BY SHANAE JOHNSON

Shanae Johnson was raised by Saturday Morning cartoons and After School Specials. She still doesn't understand why there isn't a life lesson that ties the issues of the day together just before bedtime. While she's still waiting for the meaning of it all, she writes stories to try and figure it all out. Her books are wholesome and sweet, but her are heroes are hot and heroines are full of sass!

And by the way, the E elongates the A. So it's pronounced Shan-aaaaaaaa. Perfect for a hero to call out across the moors, or up to a balcony, or to blare outside her window on a boombox. If you hear him calling her name, please send him her way!

You can sign up for Shanae's Reader Group at http://bit.ly/ShanaeJohnsonReaders

Also By Shanae Johnson

The Brides of Purple Heart

On His Bended Knee

Hand Over His Heart

Offering His Arm

His Permanent Scar

Having His Back

In Over His Head

Always On His Mind

Every Step He Takes

In His Good Hands

Light Up His Life

Strength to Stand

The Rangers of Purple Heart

The Rancher takes his Convenient Bride

The Rancher takes his Best Friend's Sister

The Rancher takes his Runaway Bride

The Rancher takes his Star Crossed Love

The Rancher takes his Love at First Sight

The Rancher takes his Last Chance at Love

The Rebel Royals series

The King and the Kindergarten Teacher

The Prince and the Pie Maker

The Duke and the DJ

The Marquis and the Magician's Assistant

The Princess and the Principal

www.ingramcontent.com/pod-product-compliance
Lightning Source LLC
Chambersburg PA
CBHW060751210726
48292CB00014B/2759